The Houses and Other Stories

The Houses
and
Other Stories

vcabotwood

The following stories appeared previously in *little stories of long ago* by vcabotwood ©2012 Virginia Cabot Wood:

Caveat: Adde Parvum Parvo Magnus Acervus Erit
Daylight Saving Time
Technology
One Day at the Pumping Station
The Dinner Party

Antarctica appeared previously as well.

Cover design by Vinsula Hastings
Softcover version printed and bound in the United States of America
Softcover ISBN: 978-1-54392-511-1
eBook ISBN: 978-1-54392-512-8

34 Main Street #6
Amherst, MA 01002
413-253-2353
www.modernmemoirs.com
White Poppy Press is an imprint of Modern Memoirs, Inc.

Contents

Acknowledgements   *vii*

The Houses   1

Caveat: *Adde Parvum Parvo Magnus Acervus Erit*   137

Angst   151

Daylight Saving Time   159

Technology   163

Joe   169

What's in a Name?   175

One Day at the Pumping Station   183

Antarctica   195

The Dinner Party   207

Hair #2   225

Subtraction   229

Acknowledgements

To all my scribbling friends, keep on scribbling.

And to Ali, Kitty, and Vinsula, thank you!

I'd like to thank my cousin Charlotte McElwain Starr for her influence and diary accounts, referenced in "The Houses" as Eleanor's encounter with gypsies and her studies in Florence.

The Houses

Chapter 1

Pat

The minute I walked into her apartment, I sensed a story. I asked my friend, "Why do you have all those pictures of houses on this wall?" I pointed to a neatly hung series of images of houses in various media—photos, paintings, even a woodcut print—that took up an entire wall of her small home.

"I really don't know," she said, "except that each picture reminds me of a different phase of my life. I moved many times and when I did, I either painted a picture or photographed it before I left. I'm especially fond of the woodcut that my daughter Susie made for me when she was in high school. Houses have so many stories to tell."

I peered closely at the woodcut and saw that it was a big old Victorian mansion. I thought it looked spooky because it was a dark, gloomy gray, but I didn't mention it.

Eleanor is my new friend. She said she's had her ninetieth birthday, but hasn't told me more. She lives in a pleasant apartment in a retirement complex. She doesn't drive a car, said she gave driving up years ago.

I recently decided, after retiring from a school where I'd worked for ten years, to be a volunteer driver for elderly people, taking them around to doctor's appointments, social engagements and the like. I've never had time to volunteer like this before, and an organization that organizes volunteer drivers said they'd pay for my gas, which was just fine with me.

My friend must once have been very good to look at—and for her age, she still is. She's stayed slim, her posture is still straight, she has a head full of dazzling white hair and her face is remarkably unlined. It's her eyes, though, that are really remarkable, and I think my eyes are strangely like hers, neither brown nor green but somewhere in between. When Eleanor is annoyed or aroused, those eyes flash a distinct warning, and one has to take a deep breath and step back quickly. Her eyes can register undeniable disapproval even though she hasn't said a word. To be truthful, it happened to me once or twice and it put me in my place for sure. And ME, once a lawyer.

After our first drive together, we cemented a real bond. After that, she always asked for me, and now that she has my telephone number, she doesn't even bother to call the company, and gives me a sizable tip instead. Which is nice, because I pride myself on my appearance; I like clothes and enjoy dressing in up-to-date fashions, even though I am retired, and her tips help me out.

I fully enjoy being with Eleanor. In addition to those pictures of houses on the wall, her apartment is crammed full of mementos, such as miniatures of people and animals collected from her travels. A row of colorful glass paperweights line up on one window sill. She has some interesting antique furniture and a couch on which she has placed bright needle-pointed pillows that she made herself. My favorite item is an enormous bird cage, shaped like a Japanese pagoda, that sits in her west window. Within it is a flourishing Boston fern.

"You might think this place is overstuffed," she said, that first time I met her as she saw me poking and peering at her things. "Most of my friends think I should get rid of a lot of it, but I can't. Everything means something to me, and since I've lost so many friends and relatives, these things are reminders of them and the times I was with them." She sighed, and then suddenly asked, "Do you want more tea?"

Whenever I visit her, she offers me that horrible, smoky Lapsang Souchong stuff that she and her neighbors here seem to favor. Once, I brought my favorite Darjeeling tea for a change, but she refused to use it. Instead, she put her loose Souchong into the teapot. In time, she poured out the tea into beautiful Spode tea cups. "The only way to have tea," she said, handing me my tea bag. Embarrassed, I stuffed the little tea bag into my purse.

One afternoon, I met Anna, one of the older women living in this complex. She came flapping into Eleanor's apartment in clothes that looked as if she'd found them in the Salvation Army discard barrel. Eleanor hadn't told me she was coming, and she's in the habit of leaving her doors unlocked. Anna stomped into the living room on a cane—she's a tall, skinny woman—and seeing us, pointed her cane at me and in a gravelly voice squawked at Eleanor, "Who is this woman, El? I've seen yuh with her a couple a times, she doesn't live here, does she? Ah surely hope not!"

"Calm down, Anna," said Eleanor. "Her name is Pat, and no, she doesn't live here. But she drives me anywhere I want to go...maybe she could help you, too."

"Well! No thank yuh! These people are totally unreliable. Ah'm surprised at yuh, Ellie!" She turned and flapped out the door without even saying goodbye to her friend.

Eleanor was quick to apologize to me. "I'm so sorry, Pat. Anna is basically a good person but she comes from South Carolina and seems never to have gotten over her old prejudices."

I've learned to get over racist insults like Anna's, and now I smile at Eleanor as if I hadn't heard a word of her friend's.

We sit together often now, comfortable in one another's presence, and try to make sense of the deplorable things going on in the world, not coming to any happy conclusion. For someone her age, though, her views are liberal—she ridicules Republicans, for instance, as hapless fools who should know better. And I love those remarks she makes.

Eleanor still wonders about people. She often tells me stories about her acquaintances in the retirement community. I take it she is a bit aloof with them. "I'm not much of a joiner," she says, "but I do have a bunch of friends here who occasionally get together for a glass of wine before dinner...which is always later than most like to eat around here. We simply cannot" (and here she emphasizes the word "cannot") "get used to eating dinner before 6:30. At home it was always seven."

She tosses her chin in the air and then, turning toward me, she asks, "What about you, Pat? Where did you grow up?"

I say, "Eleanor, I don't know much about my birth because I was adopted from an agency by two wonderful people, Julie and Lance, who couldn't have children of their own. My early years up in northern Vermont—you know it's called 'the Kingdom,' don't you? Anyway, those years with them were blissfully happy. I had no siblings to fight with, but I had lots of imaginary friends with whom I played spring, summer and right into the fall— under a row of huge fir trees that grew in our backyard. I still remember arranging parties for them when I was really little, probably not in school yet. I would make a table from a large flat rock and around it arrange chairs made from smaller rocks for my imaginary guests to sit on. Some were covered in moss, those were for the older people that came, to make them more comfortable. And I concocted delicious mudpie dishes that I put in milkweed pods for them to eat."

"What an imagination!" Eleanor comments, smiling at me. "But when it came time for school, what did you do, did you go to the public school there?"

"Yes, I did," I say, "and it wasn't much of a problem. People there were nice to me, and Julie made sure I finished my homework every night so that I could get into a good college when the time came." Julie was a teacher and a good education was important to her.

"Even so," says Eleanor, "this could not have been all that easy. How many black friends did you have, way up there in Vermont?"

"In my school, I was the only black," I say, "but most of my classmates were friendly and fun. Except for one big bully, Hank." And I actually shudder, thinking back to that one episode that occurred so long ago.

It is as if Eleanor has read my mind. "Pat," she says, "I hope you'll want to tell me more, won't you?" And she fixes those brownish greenish eyes on me, waiting for what I would say.

Chapter 2

Eleanor

"I refuse to tell you one more word about me," says Pat, pointing her finger at me like an old-fashioned schoolteacher. She is in my ancient rocking chair, which she seems to have chosen as her favorite seat in my apartment. "That is, until you tell me about you."

"There's really not very much to know about me," I say, quickly comparing my life to what Pat has told me so far about hers. "Even though I've traveled some. But I've never lived in exotic countries like many who live here. Nor, in fact, did I have any kind of celebrated career. I only got through high school. But I did manage to earn my own way when it became necessary for me to do so."

"Well, then, tell me your story," says Pat. "I love to hear other people's stories. In fact, I've spent a good part of my life listening to other people's stories. That's what lawyers do, you know."

I say, "Well...I bet I can tell you all you'd want to know about me in about five minutes," and then ask Pat if she wants another cup of tea. She nods vaguely. I can see she still is not exactly fond of my tea, but politely

9

holds out her cup while I pour more in it.

"Go ahead, Eleanor." She sits back in her chair, rocking slightly.

"I grew up with what most would say was a silver spoon in my mouth," I begin. "Yes, I'm sure I was fed with a little silver spoon holding Gerber's applesauce or Pablum or whatever it was fed to babies then."

"With nursemaids and governesses and butlers all running around like all the little rich kids I used to read about," says Pat.

"I suppose so," I say vaguely, "although all I really remember about my childhood was that Mother and Daddy were not ever together. They divorced when I was only four, and Mother traveled about, finally getting married again. My older brother and I were shuttled between relatives and grandparents until we were old enough to be sent to boarding school."

"What about your father?" asks Pat. "Didn't he take some care of you? This seems a very bad beginning. Every person deserves to grow up with someone who loves them."

"That's so true, Pat. Often people forget that children of the well-to-do can just as easily be neglected as those from more modest circumstances. Jim and I were certainly examples of that."

"Go on," says Pat, looking at me as my eyes start to tear up. I have a feeling she saw the tears and perhaps was wondering what to do if I really broke down and cried.

"Well," I begin, and right away have to blow my ever-present (it seems) runny nose, "when I was about thirteen, I was sent away to a boarding school in Virginia. It was so very Southern! We girls were to be brought up as Southern belles. How we first appeared was so important! You had to wear exactly the right thing, clothes were such a mark of place. For instance, I remember Peter Limmer shoes! Every girl had to have a pair. Those shoes were made in Austria and were very expensive. They had little colored leather insets around the lacing, and I urged my father to get me a pair, and I also worked on his current girlfriend, you know he always had some famous beauty hanging around, and as a result I got two pairs, one red, one green."

"That was pretty clever," laughs Pat. "That school must have taught you a few tricks after all."

"Yes, well...maybe it was trickery, for all I know," I say. "We were being schooled to believe that the only intellectual effort necessary was to be able to carry on a somewhat knowledgeable conversation with bright boys from Ivy League schools headed for finance, the law or diplomatic posts."

"Under those circumstances you must have had to learn a foreign language, what about that? What did you learn?"

"Latin was taught, if you can believe it. French and German were also on the curriculum until the war, and then, I believe, German was dropped."

"What about Spanish or Italian?"

"I don't think they were even considered, much too ordinary, too peasant-like, probably. But the literature courses were excellent…the South is so famous for storytelling, you know, and we had some excellent teachers. I loved those courses, I took every one offered."

"And what else? Any math or science?"

I can see Pat is a bit astounded by what was once considered the perfect education for girls going someplace, that is, taking on a search for a rich, suitable husband.

"They didn't make much of an impact that I can remember," I reply. "Science might have come in under tempting recipes for your cook to make and social studies a euphemism on how to manage household help."

Pat laughs. "Oh, Eleanor, I can see you are not much of the forgiving type."

"I can't say much about that school that is complimentary. It was an old-fashioned girls' school education that I certainly hope has been phased out by now."

"What about your brother, while you were undergoing all this finesse?" asks Pat.

"Jim and I had such a nice relationship," I answer her. "He used to tease me a lot though, and called me a 'bookworm.' Oh, I can hear him now! 'C'mon El,' he would say, 'get your nose outta that book.' I always loved to read...still do...'and let's play Monopoly.' That game had just come on the market and was quite popular. And Jim was almost impossible to beat, but it was fun to try."

"You said he was older than you, how much older?"

"He was two years older than me. He was very good-looking and lots of my friends always wanted to come to grandmother's or wherever it was that we were staying... always hopeful he'd notice them. But he always seemed kind of shy and aloof, and would disappear to avoid being checked out."

I still think about my brother with sadness and hope Pat doesn't see my eyes filling up again with these hapless tears. I try a more cheerful tone.

"Pat, one of the things that is still so clear in my mind were the summers we spent at Grandmother Joan's farm. We often took long walks in the nearby woods that were filled with big old trees. It was always shady and dark and cool in there...we often saw little animals and deer, and once we saw a bobcat...you know, the kind with tufted ears."

"We had them in Vermont," says Pat, and then goes on to describe a memory of her own, including seeing the stuffed catamount or mountain lion at the Vermont Historical Museum.

So I say, "Should I go on and tell you some more about my life?"

"Absolutely!" says Pat. "Sorry for my interruption."

"Well, then, I'll tell you about the most incredible scene we saw once in those woods."

Pat gets up and looks out the window, saying, "Go on...what did you see? Ogres, fairies, unicorns..." and laughs a little, settling back in the rocker. She is still interested in my tale.

"None of those. However, Grandmother told us about a bunch of gypsies who came every fall to gather mushrooms and always asked if they could camp in her woods while the mushrooms were in season. One day we came upon the gypsies, something I will never forget."

"Gypsies!" says Pat. "I thought they lived in Romania or someplace like that...I never knew we had gypsies in the USA." I can tell that this really piques her interest.

"We did. When I was growing up...and this encampment in Grandma's woods was a sight to see! Perhaps about sixty people, singing and dancing and celebrating. The music came from accordions and guitars and little flute-like instruments and tambourines and drums. The women were dancing around in billowing colorful skirts even while they tended cooking pots over the fires. The men wore red cummerbunds and had tied red kerchiefs about their necks. There were lots of children and dogs playing about. But while we were watching, we thought we were well concealed by trees, a surprising thing happened—a lovely, slim young woman came over to where we were standing, she'd seen us, and she grabbed Jim's hand...urging him to come and dance with her.

"She had the most beautiful face, surrounded by black ringlets of curls cascading down her back—and I think, if I had not been there, Jim would have gone with her to the firelight. I'll never forget this scene. We tried to find them another year but we were never able to. I always thought Jim would have run away with them... he had a look on his face that I'd never seen when that girl came up to him."

"That's quite a story, Eleanor. Where is brother Jim now?"

"Pat, Jim is dead. He was sent away to an almost military school—a boarding school he hated. Dad couldn't stand him, thought he was a sissy, that he needed toughening up."

Pat gasps, "Fathers do that too often, I've seen too much of it. So what happened?"

My eyes are beginning to water again. Instead, I blow my nose.

"Oh Pat! All my brother Jim wanted was warmth

and comfort, and he never got it. As a younger sister, I tried cheering him up, to make him feel better about that wretched school, the worst place he could have gone to."

"And why?"

"One morning they found him," I say. "Jim had hung himself from a bar in the school's gymnasium."

"Oh my God, Eleanor, how awful for you!" Pat gets up and comes over to put her arms around me, and then the tears really start rolling down my face.

Wiping them away with a balled-up tissue that I've found somewhere in my slacks, I say, "I'm so sorry Pat, but every time someone asks me about Jim, I start to cry, and it was such a long time ago, you'd think I'd get over it."

"I don't think one could ever get over something like that, especially since you two seemed to be so close as children." Pat is looking at me intently, sitting next to me, holding my hand. We don't say anything.

Then, looking at her watch she says, "Are you OK, Eleanor, if I leave you now? Time seems to have flown by. I really should leave before the traffic becomes impossible."

"Of course I am fine," I say. "It's just every time I think about my brother I get weepy. That's all."

"You are a brave and interesting woman," says Pat, getting up, "and I want to hear more about YOUR life when we next get together."

"Not until I hear something about yours," I say, still sniffing. "Which will be next time." I throw the balled-up tissue in the wastebasket and see Pat out the door.

Chapter 3

Pat's Random Thoughts

I leave my house, get into my car and head for Eleanor's. *Funny, what odd stuff comes into your head when driving alone, like little pictures, even when your eyes are on the road watching out for whatever crazy maneuvers other drivers might make, like right now, oops, that was a close one. Wake up, Pat!*

How I love my little house. How lucky I was to find it... in this pleasant suburb with a train station right up the street so I can go into the city without having to fight these monsters on the road. Remember, Pat, how scared you were when you came down from Vermont to go to Harvard, remember how Lance warned you about Boston drivers...he was so right! Massachusetts drivers seemed to hate those Green Mountain plates. They'd honk at you as if you were some kind of hick just because you were trying to figure out where you were and how to get where you were going, DAMN, look at THAT sap, in a MINI Cooper no less, going much too fast. Oh, and isn't my garden beautiful right now, can't wait for Eleanor to see it. I love to garden, to feel the dirt in my hands. No gloves, I just clean up when I'm through, thanks to Lili's wonderful gardening soap, better than Boraxo—yeah, lots better. Comes from France. Like Lili did. Poor Lili—she was a true gardener but smoked herself into a Vermont grave.

Vermont! Gosh, I'll be there soon! I love my Vermont garden, too. Well, I just plain love Vermont. I hope it won't be too late to hear the peepers. The mountain will have lost its snow, I can plant my veggie garden, now that the deer fence is in. What a job those critters used to do! Fence is buried underground—deep—to keep out woodchucks, too. Hmmm, hope Todd dug it in far enough, he's kind of slack! Wonder who will show up this summer to visit... Roger? Rob? Vicki? Wonder if Eleanor will miss me...I'll be there for three months, maybe more...but she seems to have a few good friends in that place. Oh, how I love Vermont and my little place here. So LUCKY me. I worked damned hard for my money...to be able to keep both. No one can say I didn't. Maybe I wasn't perfect, but then who is? Should I tell Eleanor everything? She thinks I am an amazing, nearly perfect person—EXCEPTION, I don't think she likes the way I dress. To say nothing about my choice in tea. But I know she knows I've overcome all sorts of difficulties she never had to face, how true is that! Once she asked me about being black, and didn't I want to find out where I came from? I really never thought about this much when growing up...Lance and Julie never brought it up, that I was different. So I never worried about it until I was much older. Assumed a lot, I guess. But I've messed up also. Eleanor would probably not believe it. Someday I'll tell her. DARN, look at that jerk, cutting right in front of me, no signal even! Well, here's the turn. I'm parking right here. I'll run up and get Eleanor...I hope she's ready, she can be so SLOW.

Chapter 4

Eleanor's Random Thoughts

What a beautiful day! I'm so happy—I'll be getting out of here soon. It's a nice place this home, but I do miss being able to step outside to smell spring. Uh-oh! Look at the time! Pat will be here soon, and I'm not even dressed. That's the trouble with being in a place like this, no need to get dressed right away. Mmm, nice warm shower though, I love the smell of this soap…sandalwood, I think. Mmm.

Now, what to put on? Oh dear, looks like I've gained some weight. I'll find out soon enough at Dr. Tucker's. Nurse will probably comment like she always does. "Why, Mrs. Riley! We've put on a little weight, haven't we!" So, who's this "we"? I always want to ask her, but don't. She's so nosy.

Probably all that eating out with Pat. Well, here's something I haven't worn in ages, purple like the crocuses outside the front door here. Pat won't think I'm totally dowdy if I put this on.

Pat! She surely wears up-to-the-minute styles, like all that fashionable stuff I see in magazines at the Hair Loft. But I don't like those low-cut blouses she wears sometimes. Décolleté was once just for evening, now it's called "cleavage," and girls are parading around in what looks to me like their underwear. Where's modesty gone anyway? Next thing men will be wearing codpieces—sex-sex-sex—all over the TV and magazines...disgusting, I say. But I suppose it's better than war. Hmmm, *well really, Pat has a gorgeous figure, wish mine was still like it once was. Oh well, when she's my age.... Now, shoes? Where's that nice pair of SAS shoes? This closet is too dark, can't see a thing. Oh, here they are! Pat and her shoes...those spikes she wore once, took 'em off the minute she came in and didn't put them on until she left, walked around in her stocking feet. She was going to tell me something, I think I remember. I bet she's had quite a life. Black girl like that who's come a long way. I wonder about her life, probably nothing like mine. She thinks I'm an elite. Hah! If she only knew. Oh, c'mon shoe, get on! Damn knee—weather must be changing. I wish they'd invent a salve that doesn't stink up the whole room. BENGAY is OK but I can't put that on when going out...*

Wonder what Pat's house is like. I bet kind of Vermonty.

Funny how things that you grew up with seem to stick around when you get old, at least with me they have. Brush your hair, Eleanor, and put on some lipstick so you don't look like a ghost. No, not that pinky one, how about nice bright red—celebrate spring! You're going out! Good! Now you look OK for today, at least for an old bird, ninety one.... Doorbell, that must be Pat. I'll let her in.

I'm ready for some fun!

Chapter 5

Pat

Eleanor needs to do some shopping out my way, so after we complete these chores, it's going to be time for tea at my house. I made some passion fruit iced tea and some of her (and my) favorite chocolate chip cookies that came from the Pillsbury Dough Boy. She won't know. They're pretty good...but loaded with calories, and both of us try to watch our intake of them.

Finished with the chores, we go up my short driveway. Eleanor says, "Oh Pat! I had no idea you were a gardener! You have quite the green thumb!" She tries to bolt out of the car to see everything, forgetting she still has her seat belt buckled.

"Eleanor! Undo your belt, and then we can take a little walk around the garden. I want you to see my hellebores before they've finished blooming."

"Forgetful old lady," says Eleanor with a wry smile. She snaps off her belt and slowly gets out of the car, leaning on her cane.

"Your little garden is truly lovely," she exclaims as she walks around, first examining the rhododendrons in full luscious pink bloom, then the giant grove of dark-blue ajuga beneath them. Some people think it's a weed, but I love it for its color and rampant way of growing. Hot summers here seem to control it...in Vermont, it does act like a weed, and people spend a lot of time pulling it out of places that overnight it's crept into. Then I think about gardening and how I really love to work outside.

"You know, Eleanor, making a beautiful garden is a real challenge, but a good one. It calls up creativity, knowledge and patience. Gardens I've been in and worked in—so many times—have saved me. They've given me peace, good health and creation during tough times," I tell her.

She looks at me a little strangely, her eyebrows raise a bit, and then she says, "You're so right, Pat. It is creativity, indeed. Of all the things I miss, living in an apartment, I think I miss gardening most. All I have now is my big Boston fern."

"That fern is a beauty," I say, "but let's go up and have some tea." I help her up the few steps onto the deck and settle her in one of my Adirondack chairs while I go in and get our tea and cookies. I can see her out my kitchen window, sitting there and absorbing the warm spring sunshine. The gentle, scented breeze brings the sweet smell of live growing things and the cheerful sounds of children across the street in the park and playground.

Eleanor enjoys the passion fruit tea! Relief, since

I wasn't sure she'd like it. And she says she's never eaten better cookies. I don't tell her that they aren't homemade since she doesn't ask.

"Pat," she says, "I'd like to go in now and see the inside of your house."

"Of course," I say, and help her to her feet, as those chairs are really hard for an old person to get out of. I hold the door open for her, and she goes in, crosses through the kitchen without even looking at the fancy Mexican tilework I had installed on the counters and backsplash. Then she stops in amazement by the door that leads into the living room. "Good heavens, Pat! I never would've thought your house would be like this! I was sure I'd see things all 'Vermonty,' since you grew up there."

"I leave Vermont in Vermont," I say. "This house represents my very own life. Lance and Julie, and my life with them, stay up there, all three of us, together in Vermont."

"Well, well," she says. "What a surprise. I can't believe all this. But it's truly beautiful...and unusual...it must have cost you—" and she waves her arms around as she looks at my African masks and baskets and statues, some in niches that were made for them, and my small but treasured collection of contemporary art.

"C'mon, Eleanor, sit here," I say, and indicate a nice comfortable armchair where she should sit before she loses her balance and falls.

She sits down and closes her eyes. "Oh my," she says. "Pat, this is really comfortable. Lots better than all those rickety old things I have in my apartment."

Then she adjusts the spectacles that are always sliding down her nose and looks at me quizzically. "You know," she says, "the last time we were together, you were going to tell me something about your early life. I do believe this time has come, especially since I am now in your house. How about it?"

"OK," I say, "but something that happened up there in Vermont when I was a girl is hardly memorable. I like to think of memorable as pleasure, and there was this one thing that surely wasn't. No. Not at all. But then, you asked me about unpleasant, racial stuff last time, and this unforgettable incident surely was."

Eleanor continues to look at me expectantly and, my voice choking a bit, I say, "Maybe I should get to know you lots better before I go into all the weird and lurid details of my life."

"Oh Pat!" she scoffs. "I'm an old lady. I've seen a lot and done a lot, some of which I'm not exactly proud of either. Now, come on and tell me. I'm sure we know each other well enough by now. This trusting relationship must not end."

She surely seems curious, I think. So maybe what I tell her about myself will be constructed into stories she can tell her friend Anna and the other residents of the home. That's OK with me. Hmmm, should I tell it with a certain amount of embroidery? Who knows, maybe that will help some of them get over their prejudices, if they have them.

And so I begin. "I was the only black girl at this small northern Vermont school, although historically, one of the first teachers' colleges in Vermont was started by a black man, a Middlebury College graduate at that. He was named Alexander Twilight..."

Eleanor interrupts. "Yes," she says, "and I've seen that huge granite building in Brownington...was that the name of the town? I can't remember. Anyway, I've been in that building he built with only the help of his ox...which, when they finished the building, was barbequed and eaten by all the celebrating folk in town, the poor animal."

"It's quite a story," I continue, "and well worth the trip up there to see that place. But that was long ago. And at my school, I was, I suppose, a figure of curiosity, although I never felt different. I did have some nice girlfriends who were fond of me. And it was such a fun place to go to school. Every Friday afternoon in the winter when the snow came, classes were dismissed so all of us kids who wanted to could go skiing. Skis were provided by some wealthy people who had second or even third homes in the town. We had to provide the rest of our equipment, but Julie had organized a sports equipment swap at the school, and I was always able to get what I needed. I loved skiing. Still do, but don't go much anymore."

"Were you good at it?" Eleanor asks. "Did you race even?"

"Some of the kids, boys mostly, used to make fun of me at first. In many ways they were quite hurtful, like saying, 'When Pat falls down, we wonder if she leaves a dirty mark in the snow...some of her black skin has washed off.'"

"Oh my!" says Eleanor. "Kids can be so mean sometimes! That remark would have made me mad as heck!"

"It did at first, but when I began to beat them—racing through tough slalom gates—they stopped and even began to cheer when we were in competition.... One of the things that I still remember, though, was a horrid, scrawled message, written in lipstick on the walls of the girls' bathroom. It said something like, 'Hear niggers ain't cool. Get them out of are scool.' The spelling was so bad it made me laugh."

"Oh Pat! You certainly were meant to be a lawyer since you could take stuff like that so dispassionately."

"That wasn't the worst of it. There was this one boy, a big hulk of a fellow—Hank, he was named—and he truly didn't like me at all. Every time he saw me, he would make nasty noises, and under his breath I could see him mouthing words like 'Go home nigger, go home to Africa, and live with your nigger folks.' And then he would leer at me and make more ugly noises. For some reason, he was never caught at this…I think if he had been, things might have gone differently."

"Why didn't the school officials do something?" asks Eleanor. "Or didn't you tell them about him?" She looks at me again over the top of her glasses.

"I told Julie about the stuff he was saying to me," I say, "but because his father was some kind of state official, she couldn't persuade the principal to haul him in. He told her Hank had to be caught saying those words to me before they could do any reprimanding. And Hank was smart enough to never be caught."

"Oh! Isn't that always the way." Eleanor pounds her fist on the arm of the chair. "So what else happened?"

"It's not a pretty story, Eleanor. Are you sure you want to hear it?"

She nods and says, "Of course."

"One afternoon, while waiting for Julie to get through with her lesson plans and other paperwork she always had to do, I was out in the playground, swinging, kind of absentminded, on one of the kiddy swings, watching the last leaves fall and make colorful patterns on the ground at my feet. It was late October, but a lovely, warm day, and soon it would be too cold to sit there, so I was really enjoying it. But suddenly these thoughts were interrupted. I was grabbed around the neck and pulled off the swing. It was Hank. He had me around the waist now and was pulling down my underpants. He threw me on the ground and got on top of me. I screamed and screamed and tried to claw at his eyes but he stuffed my mouth full of leaves, and grunting like some big pig, he raped me. Right there in the schoolyard! When he'd finished, he got off me and said gruffly, 'There, nigger! That'll show you not to stay around here! We don't need you except for what I just did.' And then, giving me a final smirk and one of his disgusting noises, he slunk off, leaving me hurt, covered with leaves and dirt where I'd tried desperately to wiggle out from under him.

"Luckily, Julie had come around the corner of the school building and saw me. I was still in shock, and she raced over to me. She was horrified and said something like, 'My God, Pat! Are you all right? No! I can see you're not!' And she bundled me into her arms and took me straight away to the hospital while I blurted out the frightening episode...sobbing, huge spasms of fear and anger, all sorts of emotions overcoming me."

"What a terrible thing to have happened to you," Eleanor says, white-faced and obviously upset. "What happened to that monster of a boy? I hope he was jailed or something?" She is fumbling around in her purse. She finds a tissue and blows her nose.

"Even now, every time I think of that Hank and what he did to me," I say, "I still get a bit angry. No, unfortunately nothing happened to him, as he denied ever doing it. Julie and Lance took him to court, but the case was dismissed. We were sure it was because of his father's political ties."

"Did you ever get even?" asks Eleanor, still perturbed. "If you didn't, maybe you still can." She gives me a conspiratorial smile. "Look at all the cases coming from those abused by boarding schoolteachers and Catholic priests."

"No, it's not worth it now. One summer I did run into him in the grocery store. He was disgustingly fat, and bald—and I don't think he even recognized me. I certainly didn't let on who I was. Maybe time has taught him a lesson or two...I have to hope so."

"Pat," says Eleanor, "I am in awe of you. It is not likely I would be so forgiving if this had happened to me." The strange, knowing smile covers her face again briefly.

"One cannot go through life in sorrow or anger," I say. "I've had to learn this. You've probably had to learn it, too. In fact, it's time that you told me some of your own story."

"What can I tell you after this! I'm exhausted for you, Pat."

I can see that my story has upset her, so I suggest

we head for her apartment and wait until the next time
we see each other for her to tell me more about her life.

Chapter 6

Eleanor

That was a week ago. Now Pat arrives at my apartment looking like a fashion model from *Vogue*. She takes off her shoes with those impossible high heels and starts poking around again, looking at the pictures of my houses. She asks, "Is this top picture, of a red house, the first house you ever owned?"

"Yes, that it was." And I am brought back to those bittersweet days when we lived there, my husband, Tom, and Susie and Rob, our children.

It is funny how Pat picks up on my thoughts right away. She may look like a fashion model but she has the intuition of a psychiatrist or even a seer. I'll bet she was one heck of a good lawyer. She says, "From your tone, Eleanor, I surmise those days, perhaps, were days you'd rather forget? Or what? Tell me. I told you about a bad time in my life, remember?"

"I remember only too well, Pat," I say, "but I would have to tell you a lot more about what went on in my life before that red house entered it."

"So tell me."

"You remember me telling you about that silly

Southern school I graduated from, don't you?"

Pat nods, and so I go on to tell her about the official debut I made at a ball. In those days, debutante balls were organized by society's grand dames for proper young ladies to be introduced to proper young men in the hopes that they both would find someone suitable with whom to spend the rest of their lives.

Thinking that Pat would like to hear all the details, I tell her, "I was dressed in a poufy, extravagant gown of white taffeta, lace and shiny beads, and I wore long white gloves."

"Kind of a uniform," Pat laughs. "I've seen pictures."

"Oh yes, pretty much, although some girls tried to look super sophisticated in slinky satin, and I noticed how most boys loved that look!"

Pat laughs, "Should I say, 'Boys will be boys'?"

I go on. "The leading society orchestra played into the early hours, I danced the whole night through, having a wonderful time, flirting and carrying on with quite a few boys I would never see again. Many of them killed in a war that was then furthest from any of our thoughts. We danced to all the current Broadway tunes by people like Cole Porter, Rogers and Hammerstein, Glenn Miller, Tommy Dorsey. Oh, I remember one of my favorites was 'That Old Black Magic.'"

Pat often amazes me with the breadth of her knowledge. "That was a wonderful tune. Keeley Smith sang it, remember her with Louis Prima?"

"*Hmph!* I like Frank Sinatra's version better," I say.

"Is that the generational difference!" she laughs. "But go on, tell me more."

"That ball was something to remember, the astounding food, the champagne that flowed like water, the whole thing quite overwhelming. That, and then the usual trip to Europe afterwards. Everything was paid for by my wealthy father of course. He never married again, but often was seen in tabloids with some beauty on his arm. I never saw him in person but once or twice a year."

"*Hmph!*" snorts Pat, and I have to laugh at her reaction.

"Yes, it wasn't unusual for those of us in that category to be either ignored or fussed over, as you'll see."

"But tell me about Europe. What a wonderful experience for you as a young girl!" Pat is always so curious.

"I went to school in Florence, a place set up to educate wealthy girls in fine arts. Florence was wonderful and so were the few Italian boys who were around—most of us girls fell for them. I'm not sure we learned an awful lot, but I did appreciate and still remember the scholarly art courses, taught by very erudite masters...it was nothing like anything I'd ever been exposed to. I could have stayed there forever.

"But along comes news that Germany has invaded Poland and is aiming towards Czechoslovakia. The school made hasty plans for evacuation and managed to get us three American girls—did I say there were three of us?—passage on a ship headed for New York. We were in steerage, but who cared. We had an outrageous time, flirting and carrying on with all of the sailors and some of the passengers all the way across. But, oh my, was it good to see the Statue of Liberty from the deck as we steamed past, as we'd been told of possible dangerous U-boat attacks from the Nazis all the way across!"

"You certainly seemed to be quite the flirt," muses Pat. "But go on with the rest of your story, life is so different now."

"Well, you certainly are an attentive listener to an old lady's remembrances."

"Maybe you should think of writing all these memories down," says Pat. "That world you grew up in is practically non-existent now. But please continue."

"OK." And in the telling, I found memories flooding back as if they'd occurred yesterday.

"So, when I came home, I found a job selling clothes at what used to be Best and Company in New York, on Fifth Avenue and East 51st. Anna, my friend—you've met her here in my apartment—and I lived together in a small apartment near Madison Avenue so we could both walk to work—Anna had a job in the Morgan Library and Museum on Madison and East 36th. Then, one Sunday, we heard that dreadful announcement from President Roosevelt about the bombing in Pearl Harbor. Anna was convinced New York would be attacked, and by then we'd heard some stories about German U-boats shooting down our blimps along the coast of Maine, and so she went back to South Carolina. My mother by then was married to a new husband, and she refused to move to the City, preferring country life on a farm in Massachusetts. She and her husband urged me to come there, as war was looming on the horizon, they said, and I would be much safer."

"Did you go?" asks Pat.

"I thought about it, I must say…but you know I'm kind of stubborn and I wanted to see how much I could do on my own. So I stayed in New York, not liking it very much—I didn't have many friends there—and after about a year, I asked them if I could come stay with them in the country, make myself useful somewhere on that big old farm. And that's what I did."

"What did you do? What kind of a farm was it anyway?" Pat is still curious, it seems.

"It was a real farm with all the usual animals— cows, pigs, sheep and chickens. My job, as it turned out, involved a lot of feeding, cleaning up after everything. There was an ancient Irishman who milked the cows. He lived in a neat little apartment in the big barn. It had a kitchen and a bath...everything! The old guy was always so grateful, I think he would've done anything for my Uncle Andy, my father-in-law, if he'd been asked."

"You never told me your mother's name," says Pat. "What was it?"

"My mother's name was Cecile. She hated that name, but I always thought it beautiful and much nicer than plain old Eleanor. Anyway, I really enjoyed country life. It was hard work, especially when winter came. But there was something so energizing about going out in the cold, sometimes so cold that my nostrils froze and my breath was like steam when I talked. But oh my! When spring finally came, the daffodils and crocuses, the apple trees in bloom—you can't beat that for glorious! The sweetest time of year." Pat agrees with me on the beauty of springtime in the countryside.

"However," I say, "nearby was a big Army base that still had a cavalry regiment, a remnant left over from World War I, I guess. And of course I met some of the officers. They were so dashing and handsome, and most seemed to have that éclat that came from being raised in moneyed families...Ivy League backgrounds that is. Several officers there used to ride over to pay visits to my cousin Sally, who lived with us on the farm after her parents, a doctor and nurse, went to Europe to help out in the war effort."

"*Hmmm,*" smiles Pat. "I think I can see trouble brewing."

"Not exactly," I say. "You should have seen those men on their horses! Like warriors they were. When we heard they were coming over, we would rush down to the river to watch them splash through as if it were a little creek. The horses loved it, though, tossing their heads as they, quite literally, dove right in.

"Anyway, Sally was as pretty as any girl could be, and it wasn't long before she became engaged to one of the cavalrymen, and they didn't wait long to be married either. But before they left, they introduced me to a tall, fascinating, blue-eyed Irishman named Tom Riley, an old friend of Sally's husband—they were both from Pennsylvania—and of course, the way things were back then, we, too, fell in love and were married out in the apple orchard one fine spring day."

"An orchard in bloom, what a lovely place to have such a ceremony," says Pat. "I hope the apple trees were doing their best for you!"

"Yes, it was a bountiful spring bloom that year— should have foretold all kinds of good luck."

"Well...did it?"

"I guess that is for another time, to tell you more," I say. "It really is your turn next for some more of your story before I continue with any more of mine."

"I like this—I think we're having fun," says Pat. "Yes,

next time I'll tell you more of mine, but it's not a pretty one like yours."

"Isn't that for me to decide?" I get up to see Pat out the door. The telephone rings and it's Anna, reminding me that we're having dinner together.

Chapter 7

Pat

This day I come to Eleanor's apartment just for a visit because she said she didn't need anything or want to go anywhere. Suits me fine, as I'm glad to find any excuse to get out of my own house—this rain seems unrelenting and I don't like being cooped up for very long.

When I walk in, I see two old ladies sitting cozily on the couch together, sipping tea and laughing. Oh, I think. It's that crazy old Anna there with Eleanor. But I'm polite. "Why Mrs. Eastman, how good to see you again. How are you doing?"

She looks up at me in surprise. I notice she hasn't changed her musty, dusty black clothes since the last time I saw her, a year ago. No, it can't be that long.

"Ellie," she shrieks, "what is that woman doing here again? You didn't tell me she was coming...now mah whole afternoon is spoiled."

She manages to lift herself up from the couch to come closer and stare at me through her ridiculous pair of little granny glasses that seem to be falling off her face or else she's fumbling around in her purse or pockets trying to find them.

She says, "Dahn...for a person like you, I must say, you aren't bad lookin' and y'all don't look like a good for nuthin' crook like so many of yuh are!"

With that, she flounces out the door, slamming it behind her.

"I'm so sorry, Pat," says Eleanor. "Anna should know better. I've told her over and over how much I rely on you, but because she's just old-fashioned South-Carolina-born and doesn't seem to understand.... Why anyone should act this way is way beyond me! But it isn't just you—she's rude to plenty of others around here, she doesn't pick on just you."

"Never mind," I say. "Believe me, I have been through much worse than an old lady yelling at me."

"Oh dear, yes. I remember only too well that awful incident you had up North."

Eleanor gets up slowly and looks in her closet for another cup, for me to have some tea. "Remember," she says, "it's your turn to let me in on some more of your past life.... Do you want some tea?"

Smiling at her, I reach into my purse and produce a bag of Darjeeling tea, reminding her that smoky Souchong is not for me. She laughs, puts her kettle on again to boil and soon we settle down in the living room while I begin my story.

"You remember that I told you how hard Julie and

Lance worked with me as a kid to finish my homework on time, get good marks and try to get along with those who had it in for me?"

"Yes, but I can't get that picture out of my mind of you being assaulted by that awful boy…it'll probably stay with me forever."

"Try and forget that for now," I say, "because I won a terrific scholarship to Harvard as a result of the care my parents gave me. The day we set off for Cambridge must have been one of their proudest days. Actually, I went to Radcliffe, but Julie and Lance called it 'Harvard' to neighbors and friends because they were so proud of me and the scholarship I was awarded. Students came from all over the U.S. and, in fact, the whole world. My roommate was Vicki, a Japanese girl from San Francisco. She told me how her parents had met at a concentration camp, where so many Japanese-Americans had wrongly been sent as possible spies. Everyone whose family came from Japan was thought of as a possible spy."

"I think you've mentioned her before," says Eleanor. "That was a sad move on our government's part, since many Japanese were already fighting in the war. Are you still friends?"

"Oh my, yes! Vicki was so smart. She's with the State Department, although she mentioned in the latest Christmas card she was retiring this coming summer. She has a husband and two grownup kids now, one already in college. Seems to be following her mother's footprints. But such wonderful times Vicki and I had together then."

"Tell me more," says Eleanor. "I wish I'd had the college experience."

"All I can tell you now is that we worked hard. There were few blacks on campus during those days and I wanted to prove that I could do the work as well as any white girl or guy. This became very, very important to me."

And then, suddenly, I remember an incident I thought I'd put out of my mind. Eleanor must have seen my expression change for she says, "What is it Pat? Your look has me scared."

"It's something that I thought I'd forgotten all about," I answer. "There was this Southern boy in one of my Latin classes. I've even forgotten his name; but he disliked me, somewhat the same way Anna does."

"Oh Pat, Anna is old and kind of set in her ways. When she gets to know you better, I'm sure she'll come around."

"I'm not sure about that," I say. "So many Southerners seem to have a built-in chip on their shoulders about us blacks being inferior, and we have to try and get used to or overlook their prejudices. I'm happy to be where I am, it's far less stressful—even though I'm sure there still is prejudice in places here."

Eleanor says, "I know, Pat. Our country certainly has its share of fools and dolts alive and well. Just read the news or listen to the TV. It's appalling! But...go on with your story."

"This guy used to sneer at me even when we were in class. There weren't many of us taking fifth-year Latin, and often I came out with marks a bit higher than his. I think that was what annoyed him.

"So one lovely spring evening after an early dinner with friends in the Square, I decided to make a detour to Lowell House, where another friend lived. There's a little street, like an alley, that runs to Lowell House, a shortcut from the square. Not many people were around. But coming toward me that evening was this guy, and he was drunk. I could tell from the way he walked, bumping into the sides of parked cars along the street. And then he saw that I was alone..."

Eleanor gasps, "Go on Pat, I hope he wasn't like that horrible yahoo Hank, the one you told me about."

"In a way he was. He stopped dead in front of me and wouldn't let me pass. He grabbed my jacket, his breath was disgusting, and said something like, 'Nigra! I can't believe you are at this school! You have no right, you need to be put in your place and screwed down hard like all of you black whores.'

"And then he tried to force me up against a car, but you know, Eleanor, how strong I am, and I was even stronger then, and it was easy to push him off his feet, he was so wobbly drunk. I left him there lying in the alley and hurried away as fast as I could go."

"Good grief!" says Eleanor. "At least he didn't do any harm to you. Physically I mean. Did you report this attack? I hope you did."

"I tried to, but really there was no one who could honestly help me. This jerk was from an old family who'd been sending students to Harvard for years and his own father was a member of the Board of Overseers, some kind of big deal there. So nothing was done, you could tell the whole affair was hushed up. I thought if anything like that happened again, I would report it to the *Crimson*, no matter who it was."

"Great!" says Eleanor.

"Right then I became an angry black woman," I say. "This was about my civil right, and I was in no mood to let it pass."

"So, what did you do?"

"I started an African-American organization, and with the university's blessing, we were given a room where we could meet. The next summer, four of us decided to go south and do what we could to help black people register to vote. We had taken instruction from a SNCC member to learn exactly what to do and what to expect, and to realize we were putting ourselves in a certain amount of danger. We were young and innocent, with no thought that any of this would really apply to us.

"One of the guys had an old Packard that once belonged to his father. There was enough room in that big old car for the four of us and all our stuff that we thought necessary to make this trip.

"Oh my, those memories! Driving south I couldn't believe what I saw, especially when we first crossed into the deep South. So many places still clutching to the Jim Crow laws, it seemed. At first we couldn't find any motels that would let us sleep there until we figured to use the white guy with us as a shill. He'd ask for a room, and then the rest of us would sneak in when the innkeeper wasn't watching and leave early in the morning before he was around.

"My impression of the South, coming from Vermont and then Massachusetts, felt like I was going backward in time. We had fun in New Orleans and spent some money on a fancy dinner there, but when we started out along Route 10 heading west, I was appalled by the lack of caring about preservation. For instance, I saw a beautiful old antebellum mansion adjoining a foul-smelling chemical factory. I wanted to stop and go in, but the guys laughed at me. 'Not likely you—or any of us—would be allowed within those halls,' they chuckled. We did stop to see the Tabasco plantation, where many of those fiery capsicum peppers grew, waiting to be bottled. There was also a weirdly beautiful salt mine, and an egret preserve with pretty but smelly birds who squawked unceasingly, and a beautiful botanical garden, full of flowering azaleas and camellias, where I saw my first alligator, snoozing in the shallow water not far from where I stood. And Eleanor, I still remember how that ugly beast winked at me as I stared at him!"

Eleanor smiles slightly and then turns serious. "Do you remember when you did this?" she asks. "I mean, what year?"

"It was the summer of 1965, I think. Anyway, it was right after the summer known by us as Freedom Summer, because President Johnson had just signed the Civil Rights Act of 1964. But it had upset many, many Southerners and they were going to do all they could to prevent—even if the law had been enacted— to prevent blacks from getting to vote...and to even go to the Democratic Convention." I hear my voice heating up, remembering what we'd endured down there.

Eleanor is sitting there like a stone. "I told you, Eleanor, about one of the guys that went with us who was white. He said he wanted to go to divinity school, but first wanted to answer the call of Dr. King, who'd suggested that we should go to the South to march, organize and try to persuade people to register and vote."

"What did you think of Dr. King?" Eleanor asks.

"I thought highly of him, in spite of all sorts of rumors going around about him that he was more interested in seeing black men develop their manhood, dignity and prerogatives than giving women any responsibility for change. There were others that we met whom I thought inspiring and unsung. For instance, when we got to some little town, we were fed and given places to sleep by some of the most wonderful women you've ever met. They even let us use their phones to call home now and then, at much risk to themselves. Those of us who wanted to call home, at least. Many of these nice women worked as maids or cooks for whites, and if those white people had known they were helping us and harboring subversives such as ourselves, they probably would've been fired—or even arrested, such was the mood down there during those awful days."

"You must tell me more," says Eleanor, "and I'm very curious about the white divinity student—do you remember his name, by any chance?"

"Yes. Of course. His name was Rob, I think...his last name I rather forget...Irish...like O'something, maybe. Terrible to forget, but names have always been a real problem for me. But in the night raid in jail, I think he may have been killed."

I see that Eleanor is visibly upset. She asks, "What do you mean by raid? Please, go on with your story, Pat." She shudders slightly and her hand trembles as she tries to sip some of her tea.

So I continue. "Some hoodlums came one night after we all had been arrested and were jailed in this small town. We'd helped several people learn how to register to vote. A policeman saw us leaving an AME church, where we'd gone to help with voter registration (they were all so anxious to have a say). This policeman was waiting outside the church, we saw him sitting there in his car.

"'Uh oh,' said Rob or someone, 'we may be in for some trouble with this guy. Let's get in our car and drive slowly away and find a place to eat. He shouldn't have any reason to stop us.'" At this point, I drink some tea, I need a break. Eleanor waves at me to keep talking.

"Hot as it was, Eleanor, I can remember the chill coming over me as I looked at this man, humped and insinuating, like a huge fat toad watching every move we made through enormous dark glasses.

"We started the engine and this was all that was needed for him to turn on his siren and roar over in front of us, blocking any progress we could make on that narrow street. James was driving, and he got out of our car to meet the officer. I heard him politely say to him, 'Yessir, what can we do for you?' Kind of like the way he'd talked to the people where we'd been.

"The officer didn't say a word. He simply smacked him on the face, saying, 'All right, you four are under arrest. Y'all have disturbed the peace. Ah'm puttin' y'all in jail, and then see what you damned Yankees can do to get yourselves outta here!' Only the way he said it sounded more like 'hyar,' and he spat on James's shoes. He told James to pull the old Packard over into some bushes by the side of the road. Then he put handcuffs on the boys and said to me, 'Awright girly, ya gotta come too. Just because you a girl done mean nothin' hyar,' and he snapped handcuffs on me. So there we were, handcuffed, really unable to do a thing."

"This is a most horrible story," says Eleanor. "So what happened next?"

"He made us, all four, crawl into the back of his car and drove only a few yards, certainly not much more, to the county jail, which was very small. He opened the door and gave us a rough shove inside. Pushing past us, he yelled, 'OK, Fred, I got us some more Yankee bums for yah to watch over.'

"The jailer, Fred, got up from behind his desk to look us over, carefully I thought. Anyway...then the policeman slammed out the door, got back in his car and gave us all a kind of salute—from his siren—as he drove away.

"We were left standing, sort of like dummies, in front of the law, which in this case was Fred. He was a kind and jolly fat old guy who found chairs so that we all could sit down. He said he'd go get us something to eat if we behaved ourselves. Not a problem, considering the handcuffs, I can tell you."

"Well, at least there was one decent person there, besides all those ladies you stayed with."

"Yes, and Fred came back with some cornbread and beans, and paper plates, plastic forks and knives. He unlocked the cuffs so we could eat, all of us noting the big pistol in a holster around his generous middle. While we ate, he told us stories about being in the Korean War with a bunch of soldiers from Maine and Vermont. How he and his buddies liked them all very much even though half the time they couldn't understand the way they talked. He made us all laugh with his imitation of a Maine accent in his Southern drawl. When we'd finished eating, he said to us, 'Sorry kids, but the law is the law, and Ah gotta lock y'all up now.'

"After locking the boys in one cell and me in the other, I could hear him sweep up the plates and utensils into the wastebasket and then sit heavily down into his chair. It wasn't long before I heard him snoring quite loudly.

"Then the boys whispered to me, 'Pat? Are you OK?' One of them said we might as well all try to sleep and then face what we must do tomorrow to get out of here. I agreed and leaned up against the wall of my cell, hoping that maybe sleep would come.

"But it didn't. And as I tried to think of comforting

things, like being back in Vermont, to ski powder on Jay, or to hear the spring peepers—I think I was in a sort of trance—this was when the hoodlums broke into the jail. By then it was dark outside and, finding Fred asleep, I could hear them taking the cell keys off the wall where he'd hung them. Fred awoke. I could hear him say, 'Oh hey boys, y'all can't...'' and then there was the sound of a gun going off. They shot Fred. I heard his heavy body hit the floor. And then, I guess, they shot out the one light in the place, which was over Fred's table. Then they opened the first cell door and tried to pull the boys out. My pals put up a terrible fight, oh my God! Eleanor, it was dreadful. I was so scared. I could hear them being slammed around, chairs being tipped over and broken, one of the hoodlums yelling, 'Hanging's gonna be next...so give the fuck up.' Awful words coming from the mouths of all of them. My pals, I could tell, were putting up a good resistance but they were no match for this bunch. I could hear it all, but was too scared to look out between the bars of my cell to watch. Then it sounded like they were being hit on their heads with some kind of blunt bat-sounding things, and then I heard someone say, 'Well, we got 'em now.' The three boys were being dragged and pulled out of their cell. But one of the locals said, 'Wait, wasn't there a girl along?'—and this fellow came over and peered into my cell. By then, though, I'd wrapped myself up into the smallest ball possible and huddled myself over in the farthest corner with my head down. 'Naw, there's no one in there,' this bum said, and went out. I could hear the door slam behind him."

And Eleanor looks at me. "I guess, Pat, that being the way you look was of some use in the dark that night."

"Yes, it surely was."

"So how did you get out, how long did you have to stay in jail?" Eleanor is taken up by my story and wants all the details.

"All I can remember about those few awful days is that after the truck drove away and it was very quiet, I had an enormous sense of loneliness, and fear came over me. What was going to happen? There I was in a town where no one knew me. Fred, the kindly jailer, probably dead on the floor outside my cell. Guilt feelings about not being able to help the others...I remember standing up and walking over to the cell door to hear if Fred was breathing, and I couldn't hear anything and couldn't see anything either, now that the light had been shot out. Well, there was a thin beam of light from a streetlight outside the window. I crept back to the hard bunk and began to cry, I couldn't stop for the longest time. And then I must have dozed off, for the next thing I knew, I was being jerked out of a kind of dreamless state by rough voices and heavy boots stomping into the jail.

"'Godamighty,' I heard someone say, 'look what we

got here, it's Fred! Fred! Oh my God, Fred's dead!'

"'Dead?' I heard someone else ask. And then someone said, 'Yah, and look, one cell door is open.'

"After a pause, two men in uniforms looked into my cell.

"'A girl's in here.' Then the cell door opened, probably with keys the hoodlums had thrown on the floor.

"'Well, girlie—what you got to say for yourself?' one uniform said to me. 'Where are your pals? How come they didn't take you with them when they escaped?'

"He was rough, pulling my arm and yanking me to my feet.

"'Hah, hah! Always thought girls were nuthin' but trouble—they must'a, too! Huh?' and he leered at me, putting his face right up to mine."

Eleanor is following my every word.

"Well. I spent most of that morning trying to explain to those men what had happened. For the longest time, they seemed to think that somehow, the boys had killed Fred and escaped. Repeatedly I told them, 'No, that's not the way it happened.' I was crying the whole time. Eventually, they did stop the interrogation. They shut me back into the cell and went off for lunch. I pleaded with them to call Julie and Lance, but they only laughed at me. 'You got no money to pay for that call and neither do we!' and slammed the door.

"As it turned out, Julie and Lance were already in

the air. One of the women who'd helped us realized that we hadn't told our parents where we were going, and that probably no one knew where we were. She called Julie and Lance—I'd given her their number and some money to pay for a call to them in case anything happened to us."

"Do you know what happened to those three young men who went down there with you?" asks Eleanor.

"No. Not really. I never saw or heard anything about any of them again. I don't know why, but I've never even tried. I could get the records of the arrest, but for some reason I haven't wanted to. Maybe I was afraid that they died from their injuries."

"How long were you in that jail?"

"I was there for a day or two before Julie and Lance arrived. I heard all about Fred's funeral, with the whole town in attendance. I was told about it by his replacement, a skinny, nervous, young deputy sheriff who only brought me food and water when he remembered.

"When Julie and Lance arrived, Lance, I swear, could have started the whole Civil War thing all over again by the words he used to get me released. Words that I never heard him use before or since. 'Miserable backwoods mutants' was one phrase I'll always remember though.

"I could see the young sheriff nervously fingering his new revolver, so big that it looked too big for him to handle. He kept insisting he had to have the law to set me free, but Lance would hear nothing of it, and finally the sheriff opened my cell door. Julie was standing next to the door and gave me a big hug.

"'OK, OK,' said the sheriff, 'get your sorry selves outta here and don't come back, yuh hear?'

"'Don't worry about that!' we all said, almost in unison, as we rushed out to the old Packard— miraculously still where we had been forced to leave it, keys and all in place—and climbed in. Lance tried the ignition, it turned over, and with relief we aimed straight for Vermont."

Eleanor looks at me sadly. "You know, Pat," she says quietly, "you were all lucky to get out. I've mentioned my son, Rob, but I never told you that for two years, I didn't know where he was. That's OK. He wanted separation from family. Well, I was always hoping he'd call or send a postcard or *something* to tell us he was all right, and where he was and what he was doing. But he never did. And...that Rob you were with, well—I'm quite sure he was my son."

Chapter 8

Eleanor

"Good morning," I hear Pat say as she enters my apartment. "What have you got on the list for us to do today?"

I hadn't planned anything much. But it's late September, and the trees are at their peak fall color, so I suggest we take a drive out into the country for some leaf peeping.

"Pat," I say, "The story you told me last week, about your work in the South to help people down there, will stay with me forever. What's so difficult for me to understand is why some people behave so horribly to others and why, especially in our Southern states, full of churches and religious beliefs so important to preachers who preach and preach and preach, there's so much violence, so much hatred...I don't get it."

Pat ignores my rant, but nods her head and says, "C'mon Eleanor, get your coat and we'll be off."

It seems as if she hasn't heard me. She's bustling about, gathering up the used cups and saucers from the living room and putting them by the kitchen sink, then helping me into my coat.

Sometimes Pat seems like some sort of army general and other times like a mind reader. Not commenting on my observations, though, is new and puzzling. Anyway, we get in her car and head west for some serious foliage viewing.

After a few miles of silence, Pat looks at me and says, "You know, Eleanor, it's your turn to tell me more of your story. I didn't answer you, back there in your apartment, on purpose. I have enormous comments to make on whatever you've been thinking about. Like they say, it would 'fill a book.' But today is a great day to tell me more of your story, no interruptions, no visitors... you can tell me as I drive along."

"I would, sometime, really like to hear your comments on this intolerance here in this country, OK? But where did I leave off in my story? After your tale, Pat, mine hardly compares."

"I think it was when you got married in the apple orchard to that Irishman who'd wooed you right off your feet, and you lived happily ever after," says Pat, laughing.

I think about this. "Well, no, Pat. It didn't exactly end that way...I'll tell you why." I wonder how much I should divulge, but since we're heading towards a town I called home for quite a few years, I decide I can at least tell her about that part of my life.

It is truly a glorious fall day, the sky a beautiful

September blue, the trees blazing red, orange, yellow and even chartreuse...a perfect day to be outside.

"So, after you were married...what happened?" Pat takes her eyes off the road to look at me briefly.

"We went to Camp Pendleton in California while Tom got special training to go overseas...and I got pregnant—with Rob. After Tom left, I came back East to stay with Mother and Uncle Andy on the farm. I tried to help, but found it difficult. I didn't feel well the whole time until the baby was born."

"That's too bad," says Pat, "You had such a good time there earlier."

"Yes, that's what I remembered, but being pregnant was no fun. Finally, he was born and he was a beautiful baby—but a cranky, fussy little fellow. I named him 'Robert,' not particularly after anyone, I just liked the name."

"Did Tom get back to see him?"

"Yes, around Christmastime. He came to the farm, we had a good two weeks together with our little fellow, and after he left, I found I was pregnant again. Baby Rob was just over a year old, beginning to walk and talk—although talking was not anything he did with ease—he was quite shy—silent and thoughtful. He reminded me of my brother."

"*Hmmm*," says Pat, "I'm assuming the new baby was daughter Susie...the apple of your eye! You've talked so much about her."

Amused, I say, "Well, she was so different. She was round and rosy with curly red hair, an easy baby to care for compared to Rob. And so curious! She wanted to get into everything to see how it worked. I can tell you I had a few nervous moments as she grew up."

"Where did you live then? You didn't say."

"When the war was over, we rented an apartment in the city while Tom attended business school. He'd applied to Harvard but hadn't been admitted. He had to settle for something else. He always grumbled about it. It was a major disappointment to him, and I think it colored his subsequent actions for a long time."

"The proverbial chip on the shoulder?"

"Yes. It always seemed to be there. Even so, he did find a good job with an investment firm, and it paid well. I could never understand his feeling of being inferior because he hadn't gotten into Harvard Business School. Anyway, we both began to think about a house in the country—a good place for the kids to grow up and for us, especially for him, a chance to dispel the gloom. Besides, the apartment was getting cramped for the four of us. So we went on a house hunt with a friend who'd gone into the real estate business."

Pat looks again at me. "The first house in the collection of pictures in your apartment, I believe, is a pretty old colonial. It's at the top. Am I right?"

"You are. Moreover, thinking back now, this was one of my favorite houses. In addition, they were busy, fun-filled years...until Tom's accident. Then such sadness, frustration. This is what I remember now."

"Keep remembering, Eleanor. No, wait, let's stop here for lunch. This looks like a nice place." Pat pulls into the parking area of a cheerful-looking restaurant, and we go inside.

I order a cup of very good clam chowder and a BLT, and Pat has corn chowder and a hot dog with all the trimmings. Then, over coffee, she urges me to continue with my story. As I relate it to her, memories come flooding back, one on top of another...funny, sad and difficult as they were.

I tell her about the first happy years we lived in that old colonial. Old houses appeal to me. I guess it's thinking about the years of the many souls who lived there, the integrity of the builders, the sturdiness of the building that has withstood storms of nature without and storms of people within, and remains standing.

I remember the patterned wallpaper we put up to cover the horsehair that poked through the plaster here and there. I remember stenciling the white walls of the front hall, which Tom had so carefully painted, with a colonial pattern I'd found in the town library.

"We did much of the repair work by ourselves," I say.

I notice that we're near where this house once

stood, but houses have popped up like mushrooms after a rainstorm throughout the area, and I can't figure out exactly where it had been. A Pete Seeger song goes through my head, all about little boxes, meaning subdivisions with little houses. When we lived there, it was all pasture land and woods.

"But isn't that half the fun of home ownership? I did a lot to my own house," Pat interrupts.

I'm lost in my own thoughts, though. "Uh, let's see.... Our house sat up on a small hill overlooking a lake, such a pretty lake. In the summers, we had picnics down at the shore on a nice sandy beach. The water was never muddy or smelly, and stayed on the cool side because it was spring-fed."

"Oh, how wonderful!" Pat says and smiles encouragingly. "I wonder if we could find that lake."

"I also grew a big vegetable garden, and some evenings kids and their parents would come to our beach to swim, and we'd cook hamburgers and hotdogs and s'mores...usually ending the evening by singing songs like '99 Bottles of Beer' or 'Row, Row, Row Your Boat.' Always such fun.

"But Tom...Tom would join us to eat and he'd stay for a while, but then he always said he had business to attend to, and he'd go back in the house. No one ever said anything to me about this, but I'm sure some wondered about him."

Pat smiles. "Maybe you'd rather not find that old house. I can see by your expression...some memories are not so great."

I make a kind of weird noise. "No, I sort of would love to see it. On the other hand, people say you can't and shouldn't try to go home again. It would be disturbing to see what the new owners might have done, if it's still there at all. For me, it's bad enough to see all these houses! The fields and woods where Rob and Susie had such fun...all gone." I sit there, becoming quite the surly passenger.

We drive along in silence. "The catalyst," I finally continue, "to making a move was actually the June 1953 tornado that caused huge damage in Worcester, and we, halfway between there and Providence, felt a lot from it. Detritus was spread all over our yard."

Pat says, "I guess I was alive then, but in Vermont probably. And too young to know anything about it. What do you remember about the tornado?" Suddenly, she slams on the brakes. "Eleanor! Look through those trees! I see blue water!"

Yes, she's right. Through the red and yellow leaves, I can see our little lake, but we're on the opposite side of where our house used to be.

"Pull on up a little," I direct her. "That's where the public parking was."

Now I'm excited to see our lake. I remember it still,

with fondness.

We walk down to the shore, where the lake sparkles in the bright sunlight. The trees surrounding it and reflected in it are a glorious patchwork of color, interspersed with an occasional dark green of pine or fir, a palette I'd enjoyed here so many times. Above us, puffy white clouds sail by, pushed along by a gentle breeze.

"This is wonderful!" says Pat, as she skips a stone along its surface. "Lance showed me how to do that!" she says, seeing my surprise. "We used to go fishing a lot together."

We walk along the shore to a comfortable-looking bench and settle on it. It is quiet all around us until Pat urges me to continue telling her about the tornado, and I re-enter the memory of it. "It was such a long time ago, Pat, but that June day was unusually hot and humid. I'd listened to Don Kent, our favorite weatherman on the radio, and he'd predicted heavy afternoon storms with thunder and lightning.

"The kids were down at the lake when I heard the first rumble, and soon they came running up to the house, without me even calling them in. A strange wind had begun to blow hard, and the pelting rain was being swept sideways by it. The sky had darkened and was turning an eerie yellow.

"We ran into the house, madly running around to

shut windows tight and to make sure our dog, Rover, and the cats were inside. The thunder got louder and there were fierce lightning strikes; one hit something near, and I heard the blast and then the sizzle. I tried not to show any fear, as I didn't want my kids frightened, but it was hard, I tell you!"

"Gosh," says Pat, "You paint quite a picture, even now. Weren't the kids scared anyway?"

"Susie was fascinated by the storm. Only about five, she stood at a window, admiring the way odd things were blown by.... I remember once she cried out, 'Look, look... newspapers...someone's panties...a sweater! What's happening, Mama?' She seemed fearless."

"I finally made her get away from the window in case something should blow it in and break glass all over her. Besides, with every gust of wind, that old house creaked and moaned.

"'Well, this is quite a storm,' I remember saying to them, trying to stay calm as the lights flickered and then went out. We were in the dark save for a flashlight that I sent Robby to get in a side table drawer in the living room. Fortunately, it was in working order."

"Where was Tom all this time?" Pat is scuffing her shoes in the sand. This time the shoes are sensible flats. She decides to take them off and wiggles her toes in the sand. "This sand is still nice and warm," she murmurs. "Please, go on with your story."

"I tried phoning Tom at work, but it was too late, as the phone had gone out, too. So we waited, hoping to hear from him after the storm cleared away.

"After some time, the moon came out and the clouds disappeared, and the sky looked beautiful from the house. I stepped outside to see what damage had been done. For one thing, there was a huge truck tire in my herb garden. No doubt, I thought, we'd find lots more the next day."

"Did Tom show up?"

"No, he didn't. The telephone truck finally came down our street, and after repairs were done, I called Tom's office. His secretary answered.

"'You don't have Tom with you?' she asked. 'No. He's not here. And we haven't heard from him. There was a terrible storm out here, you know.' 'Heard all about it,' she said, 'the news is full of it.'

"She promised to call me if she heard anything or if Tom showed up. So then I hung up, very, very worried."

"That must have been awful," Pat says supportively.

"It was. I remember going about cleaning up as much as I could outside with the children helping me. We sat down to a cold supper, as the electric power wasn't on yet. The kids finally went to bed and I sat up in a chair near the phone, hoping it would ring. I fell asleep in the chair, woke up after a bad dream in which Tom never came home, but finally went to bed.

"Two whole days later we got news. The call came from a nearby hospital where they had Tom. The police had brought him there. Apparently, in the storm, his car had gone off the road, the windshield badly damaged. Tom had been hit in the head by a flying piece of tree or something. He'd been driving home."

"How terrible for you. What did you do then?"

"We scrambled right away into the car and headed for the hospital as quickly as we could. I remember someone telling me it was so important for a family member to be present as much as possible to mentor the situation for the hospitalized patient. When I got there, I demanded to see the doctor in charge and was told I had to wait, as he or she was operating. The kids and I were ushered into a small room to wait for the doctor. I still see the picture of Robby, all hunched over in one of those hard plastic chairs, trying to hold back tears, as he worshipped Tom from afar, even though for the most part, Tom never gave him, his own son, very much time or attention."

"And Susie? What was her reaction to all this?"

"Susie was Susie!" I reply. "She stood in the doorway and pestered everyone walking by who wore a white coat. 'What's happened to my daddy?' she would ask each one. Some would smile and say, 'Honey, I'm so sorry, I don't know.' Others would walk by, not even looking at her.

"On my own inquiry, I did finally find out that Tom's head was being examined and a small operation was being performed...it wasn't as bad as it could have been...the doctor would be out soon and would tell us."

"He didn't die then?" asks Pat. "You told me that he died a long time ago."

"No, he didn't die then," I answer. "We brought him home with strict orders to keep him quiet until all wounds healed, and even after that, with hospital visits to make sure all would be well."

"So how did that go?" Pat is putting her shoes and socks on, but sure wants to know the details of everything, so it seems.

"When Tom came home, he was not the easiest patient, let me tell you! I had a hard time keeping him comfortable and in a decent mood. In fact, I'll tell you about one incident that illustrates this and a real reason to cause us to make a move."

"Go ahead," says Pat, looking at the lake. "What happened then?"

"During his convalescence, Tom used to sit in the living room reading—but more than reading, he mostly looked out the front window, where he could see all the comings and goings along our small street. Not much usually went by except farmers on tractors, the school bus and, occasionally, a car or two. That day, I'd made an especially tasty soup from fresh garden vegetables, and homemade crusty bread that was his favorite."

"That sounds pretty good," says Pat.

I turn to look at Pat. "He was so nasty, Pat! He picked up a spoonful of soup after I'd set the tray down on a folding table in front of him, and then said, 'Why in hell, Eleanor, do you always have to make the soup so damned hot?' He then grabbed the bowl and threw it at me. It splattered all over me, the floor and the nice new carpet his mother had given us. He tried to get up, but he couldn't make it, and sank back in the chair to sullenly stare out the window. I went upstairs and changed my clothes, then I picked up the mess and cleaned the carpet. When I was done, I went outside. I had to get away from the house and from Tom, who'd fallen asleep in his chair. I was in tears, I remember it well."

"Difficult days to be sure." Pat gently feels for my hand and gives it a squeeze, and we sit quietly together, looking at this tranquil scene, thinking about Tom after the tornado.

"Yes, some of them were. But another thing happened. It was after Tom had gone back to work. But you know...I don't think his head was ever truly healed even then.

"You asked me once what made us move from our beloved first home. Well, it was a bad commute for Tom and our kids needed a change. One day, when Rob and

Susie came back from school, Rob's face was bleeding and he had a black eye. Susie's clothes were torn. I asked them, in horror, I might add, 'What happened to you two this time?' They'd both been in scrapes with other kids before, but nothing like this. My kids stood there in front of me, tearfully relating what had gone wrong.

"Apparently, Susie had been ganged up on by a bunch of kids who didn't approve of her tomboyish ways. Yes, she was a tomboy, loved climbing trees, playing baseball, investigating the woods, the lake—and these kids thought she was queer and started taunting her. Robby went to her defense, and got beat up as a result."

"Where were all the grownups in this fracas?" Pat asks a sensible question.

"From what the kids told me, it took place just as all the school buses were rolling up, the teacher's distractions were elsewhere."

"So did you report this to the higher-ups anyway?"

"We did. But there were unfortunate subsequent problems, and they became the catalysts to making a move to a more enlightened community. We found one a bit later, a fine old house in a progressive suburb just outside the city."

"Oh! I know that house, the old gray Victorian right under the red house—is that the one?"

"Yes, indeed, that's the one. But, Pat, I think we should go home now. I'm getting a bit chilly."

So we head back to the car. All in all, even with bringing back those old, bad memories, it has been a superb day to be outside.

Chapter 9

Pat

After that delightful afternoon in the country, this week I have Eleanor at my house. She wanted to get out of the apartment. She says sometimes she gets claustrophobia in there and needs to see the real world outside. But now she's pestering me for more details about my life, so to humor her I continue, remembering details that I haven't been able to forget.

"You asked me about life after that trip down South, Eleanor. I have to say, some of it, I'm not exactly proud of. One was I met a handsome dude named 'Al.' Oh, my, yes! He was very good-looking and he certainly knew he was! He'd been a football star at a university in South Carolina, but what I didn't know, at first, was that he was a confirmed druggie. He paid me such wonderful attention...and it was through him that I lost it."

"Lost what?" Eleanor's smile is wry.

"My virginity." (Of course Eleanor had already figured that out.) "He was so charming, so persuasive, and I had such an attraction for him that I simply couldn't help myself."

"And so, I suppose you got pregnant?" It'd be hard to

surprise Eleanor.

"I'll have to admit that, yes. After some really hot sessions, I found myself in that condition. I was *so* afraid. But I decided to call Julie and tell her what had happened. I was plenty scared of what she would say—she always was quite a strict disciplinarian, and I wondered how she would take this news."

"I hope she was sympathetic. Young people often make mistakes like that. It's how we learn."

"She was wonderful, Eleanor. She told me to go to the nearest Planned Parenthood clinic and talk to them about what I should do. It was one of the most difficult experiences of my life, but the people there were kind and reassuring. And I had some conversations with Al, and he turned out to be not the least bit interested in my plight. So I had an abortion, not exactly painless either."

"Oh! How sad, how very, very sad." Eleanor wipes her eyeglasses on her shirt as if this will make her see better. "I'm not exactly pro-choice, but I do feel that every woman should have the right to choose what she should do with her own body, especially under circumstances like you were in."

"There was no question about what I should do at the time. I knew what was right. And when it was all over, Julie came down to be with me over a weekend. I'll never forget the love and support she gave me then.

She and Lance have made all the difference in what was and is my life."

"Your Julie certainly seems to be one wonderful person. But what did you do with that dreadful boy, Pat? You sure have had your fill of difficult and nasty males!" Eleanor wipes her eyeglasses again.

"Yes, I surely did when I was younger. Then after some time went by, Al came sniffing around again like some hungry old dog. But he got nowhere. I told him in no uncertain terms that I would have nothing more to do with him or his druggy pals, and if they did bother me, I'd call the police and tell them what he really was. I think I scared him—I was really ferocious—and he took my advice and stayed away."

"Did you ever go back to that area, wherever it was that you got into trouble?"

Eleanor is so curious about all this. Why?

"Well, yes, I did. I was back in school, living in Cambridge, and started working in one of those poor places there, tutoring children in those sad schools and through the Boys and Girls Club there, and I started a theater group there, too. We put on plays that some of the kids had written, and the last play of the season was always something by Shakespeare. It was successful, if I do say so myself! The waiting list to get into the program was enormous. Besides doing all of that, I started concentrating on getting my marks up again. By the time graduation rolled around, I was told I would graduate magna honors. Not summa, but hey, magna was good enough for me."

"All of that must have looked terrific on your resume." Eleanor gives me a big smile. *I hope it doesn't sound like bragging, but all of it is true. How on earth did I have all that energy?*

"Well, after graduation I continued in that sad area with another venture. I saw how those kids were eating—mostly chips and junk food—when they came to school, so I decided that they needed to know about eating properly. I found a vacant lot and started a vegetable garden with a few interested parents. These parents were thrilled. They remembered about their grandparents' gardens down South, full of greens that tasted so good. They sent for seeds and we started to grow them in the lot. And then some suburban garden club ladies got wind of this project and brought bags and bags of compost. I think those garden club ladies got some significant views of poverty, which they knew nothing about, by working alongside those city dwellers who, honestly, had so little."

"You were Michelle Obama before Michelle Obama," says Eleanor, "and I'm so happy to hear all this. You were...and are...something quite wonderful!"

Eleanor gets up out of the chair with difficulty and gives me a big hug. It's awkward for her, and her glasses fall off her nose onto the floor. She almost loses her balance trying to pick them up. I get them for her and am touched by this rare show of affection.

"Such revelations, Pat," she says, "but I suppose I should be getting home. I hate to have you drive in the dark, now that the days have shortened up so." She looks at her watch.

"I don't mind driving in the dark...yet," I say, "and I still have some things to get off my mind. You're a very good listener, you know."

"In that case," Eleanor replies, sitting down again, "go on. Graduation and such...."

"Well, yes. Julie and Lance came down for the ceremony, which, as you know, Harvard makes quite a thing of. After the ceremony, they took Vicki Lee, my roommate, and her parents to dinner at Locke-Ober's, that fancy old Boston restaurant, where we all ate lobster and laughed a lot."

"And in the fall you went to law school?"

"No, not right away. I went home to Vermont for the summer and helped Julie and Lance with their huge vegetable garden. In fact, they put me in charge of it, and it was back-breaking work at times, especially when the temperature rose and the humidity with it. I bought a booth at the local farmers' market and sold our extra produce, and it was actually fun. Part of the fun was seeing people I hadn't seen since I'd gone away to college."

"No awful Hank, I hope."

"Not a sign of him."

"OK. Now tell me about law school."

"I was accepted at Harvard Law, but I stayed only one semester—"

Eleanor interrupts. "Wow, that's something unusual. So many are so proud of their Harvard Law School degrees. Real feathers in so many caps! So what happened to you there?"

"It just wasn't for me. After being with those people at that school...oh, so many of them were so avaricious that I decided that this kind of life—corporations, taxes and things being taught with the underlying feeling of making tons of money by legal approaches to tax evasion and the like—wasn't what I wanted. In a way, it really sickened me."

"Well, then, what did you do?"

"When I left, I went south again, and taught school in South Carolina. The school I was sent to was on a barrier island off the coast, with a sizable black population and a rickety school building, for pupils up to grade eight. I was put in charge of a sixth-grade class. I think my students and I got along pretty well. I introduced them to writing plays, putting on dramas for the whole school to watch—I introduced math concepts by building scenery, fashion and art were learned by creating costumes. We really had a good time for two years. And then we got a new principal. The old one had to be replaced, as he spent most of his time in his office drinking, which was why he never bothered me and my unconventional way of teaching. But some of the other teachers had figured out about him and they'd demanded a replacement. When she came, there was no more teaching the way I was doing. She ran that school like a jail, she felt these kids couldn't advance and there was no use teaching them anything more than obedience."

"Maybe she was jealous of your success with them, too," says Eleanor. "Did that Harvard degree impress her?"

"No. And I think with that woman, it actually was a deterrent. I knew she made remarks to some of her teacher buddies about what a snob I was because of my Harvard degree, which I'd always tried to downplay. The thinking there was so retrogressive that I decided to hand in my resignation, and applied to the Vermont Law School, which specialized in environmental law. I was accepted."

"*Hmph*,' Eleanor sniffs. "Such an interesting choice! And one I like. Good for you! Just look at what some recent Harvard Law School graduates have done! That Citizens United thing...the worst decision ever made since Dred Scott!" Her face has turned red, I can tell this is a sore point with her. What a wonderful old provocateur!

"Yes, Eleanor. But that school also produced Obama, and you said you liked him."

"*Hmph!*" She's still angry. "True enough, but what can he do with idiots like Mitch, who claimed he'll allow Obama only one term as president, and those other politician impediments." Her nose goes up in the air, and she raises her arm as if to slap these offenders. "These awful people should be hung and quartered!" she sputters. Then she blows her nose and wipes her glasses.

"Well, what did you study?" she finally asks, once she's simmered down.

I reply slowly, not looking at her but out the window, where it's become late afternoon and the shadows on the lawn have grown long and dark. "I had a wonderful, eye-opening experience there. We had the fundamentals of law early on, and then we could kind of customize our education to build the skills necessary to practice law in the areas of our own interests...like solving community problems, which was what I did for a long time. I was also editor for the *Vermont Journal of Environmental Law*. I was busy with my practice for over ten years, sometimes bucking awful moneyed interests, like millionaires who wanted to build monuments to themselves on every mountaintop."

"What do you mean by that?"

"I mean that some rich folk wanted to build higher and higher up on our mountains, just to show off, to show off their money...kind of like that old saying, 'I'm the king of the castle and you're the dirty rascal,' something like that anyway."

"Aren't there rules about how high one can build?"

"Oh my, yes...there are. But the point was to ignore them—these people loved controversy, too. I headed a committee in one town that was very close to succumbing to a man who was going to build huge houses well above the height line that had been drawn by the state long before I got involved."

I pause for a moment while memories about that time come flooding back. I'm not sure how Eleanor will react to hearing them. Then I continue. "Most town officials in that place thought only about how much money they'd get from property taxes on those opulent homes, without thinking that they'd be opening the way to building higher and higher on every hill in every town in Vermont, ruining the views that so many people came there to enjoy, and costing the town extra money in services like roads, schools, and fire and police departments."

"Sounds familiar," says Eleanor. "Nice places to walk, to picnic, to enjoy the outdoors are becoming so scarce everywhere. It's so sad."

I think about the changes in Vermont, and here, but

what can one do other than try to save a few special places? After all, people have to have a place to live...it's the greedy ones who should somehow be checked.

"It's time for me to go home," says Eleanor, looking at her watch. "I guess you and I can't solve all the world's ills, but it's fun and important, I think, to point them out. Some people never think about anything unless it has to do with themselves."

A knot in my stomach starts to form again; greed still angers me. Indeed, I should take Eleanor home now.

Chapter 10

Eleanor

Today, the woodcut of our old gray Victorian house seems to have caught Pat's attention again. She looks at it while I make the tea and put it on a tray with cups and saucers, and take some cookies out of their packaging and put them on the tray, too. In this place, I don't do much baking, and I've noticed that Pat doesn't do much either: We ate Pillsbury cookies at her house the other day.

"You have to tell me about this," says Pat, pointing to the picture.

I think back. "Yes, those last two years were difficult. After enduring the tornado, we experienced several crippling blizzards, one of them so ferocious that we were marooned in the house for almost a week. The snow was so deep and heavy that it took time for the town to get to our road and plow us out. We kept the house warm by stoking our fireplaces—there were four—and drawing water from our spring-fed well. The water was always cold and delicious.

"After some neighborhood goodbye parties, moving day arrived, and we all cried real tears on leaving this place of memories. Sadly, we followed the big moving truck with all of our possessions into the suburbs. The first night there, I remember so clearly. We ate dinner at a restaurant a few minutes from our new house. We'd never done this when we lived in the country, as there weren't any restaurants for miles around."

Laughing, Pat asks, "And how about Rob and Susie? Did they adjust OK? Sometimes moving is very hard on kids."

"It's supposed to be hard on everyone," I say. "I read somewhere that after death and divorce, moving can be number three traumatic."

"Was it difficult for you? Or Tom?" Pat is so curious. "Anyway, I should think the commute into the city must have been far better for him."

"For the first several years, we had no trouble. In fact, the kids were delighted with their new situation. Susie loved her school, pleased and amazed that no one found her different because of her ways. There always seemed to be tons of kids down in the basement, where we'd fixed up kind of a studio/playroom for them; she had a million projects going, she was really quite artistic."

"What about Rob? Did he adjust as well as Susie did?"

"Not like Susie. But he was pleased with his new teachers, said they really knew their 'stuff,' as he called it. Not like the ones he'd left behind. He thought they'd always been unfair to him."

Pat says, "If he was the one that went with us to the South as a divinity student...he had some pretty interesting ideas even then."

"He did. He wrote poetry that he kept hidden from us. I found it after he left with you all, and was dismayed by its sadness. The trouble was, as Rob became a teenager, he became total anathema to Tom. He could do nothing right in Tom's eyes."

I go into the kitchen to put more water on to boil, as Pat heads for the old rocking chair and sits down. "What about Tom?" she asks.

"Tom—oh, dear, poor Tom." I sigh, thinking of those last days together. "Pat," I say, "Tom realized that his health, his mental health, was not holding together. From being a pleasant, fun-loving man whom I'd married so joyfully, something had changed in him. He became withdrawn at first—remember me telling you how he'd always leave our picnics early?"

Pat says, "I remember you telling me that, indeed!"

"Well, anyway...after the move, he decided to get professional help and found a psychiatrist whom he thought was quite wonderful. Trouble was, she was smart and beautiful, and Tom fell for her."

I pour the hot water into the teapot and add the Darjeeling tea leaves Pat likes. She gets up and carries the tray into the living room, and I prepare myself to continue my story, to talk about this memory that's so enlarged in my brain. Maybe talking it out will help it go away. I sit down and sip my tea.

Pat says, "This scenario isn't uncommon, Eleanor. I've heard of other cases where this happened. But how did it affect you all?"

"Tom took his guilt feelings out on us. We weren't living up to his expectations. When he came home one day and announced he wanted a divorce, I wasn't surprised.

"I argued loud and hard for suitable alimony, since I'd be the one to take care of our kids until they could take care of themselves. I didn't mince words. Tom was not reasonable—I guess his lady love was also demanding, wanting expensive travel, dinners out and so forth. There were some pretty harsh words that flew between us...." I sigh again, remembering one particular evening that changed our lives—the kids' and mine— just about forever.

"I had no idea," says Pat, "that you had trouble like that. You always seem so serene."

"Truly. It was an ugly evening. And when Tom and I left the room, who should I find standing in the hall but Rob. He'd heard every single word between us. He told us then that he, too, was leaving. Some friends, he said, were as sick of school as he was...parental bossiness, just life in general. He was going in someone's old car to the South, maybe he'd work there, maybe he'd travel around, maybe he'd stay on an Indian reservation. He wasn't sure. But he could no longer stand living with us and our arguments. Pointing at Tom, he said, 'I hate you, Dad. You cheated on Mom, and all she's done is care for us in the best possible way. I never want to see you again.'"

"That was rather strong! And how did Tom react?"

"'That's fine with me!' he says. Then he bangs out the front door. I could hear him start up the car as he went off to the doctor's house, I suppose, to be comforted with a double gin martini and soothing words." I laugh a little. It almost seems like a story about someone else, a story that from where I stand has no ending.

"And Rob? What did he do?"

"Rob went down into the basement where Susie was working on something. I could hear him saying goodbye, and Susie crying out for him not to leave. 'Please, Rob,' she said over and over, 'please don't leave.'"

"But he did?"

"Yes. In spite of both Susie and me urging him to stay. He went to his room, finished packing a duffle bag, and that evening, without so much as a goodbye to me or Susie, he left. He was so quiet that neither of us heard him go. And it wasn't until several years later that I saw him again."

All Pat can say is, "Oh, my God!"

That was kind of my reaction at the time, I think. "But after Susie graduated from school and was on her way to college...Pat, I bet you can't guess what I did next."

"No, I can't for the life of me think what you did." Pat is shaking, her cup and saucer rattle in her hand.

"I bought an inn in Vermont," I say, astonishing her. "It was named 'The Pink Mallow Inn,' after a pretty wildflower that grows along the sides of many local roads there. And I worked there for three hard years until Rob showed up."

"And here I thought I was the only one for miles around with Vermont ties," Pat exclaims.

Chapter 11

Pat

The rocking chair in Eleanor's apartment has always appealed to me, and I go over to sit in it and enjoy its comforting, creaking motion.

"I'm going to tell you about a part of my life that I'm not exactly proud of," I announce to her. "But I did what I did with good intentions, not making any money for myself but helping Julie and Lance with their troubles."

Eleanor puts down her cup of tea to look at me over the top of her spectacles. "Pat, you and I have lived quite different lives, haven't we? But I can say, at least for me...what a trip!" She laughs softly and takes a sip of her tea. Did she hear what I said? I don't think so. I think some other thought has caught her attention.

"Yes," I say. "Indeed! What a trip! And it's not over yet."

Eleanor turns abruptly to me. "For you, probably not. But at my age, Pat...I'm over ninety, after all—my trip is nearly at an end. And I don't really care, especially since the world, our little blue planet, is in such a mess, and I see no way out, especially since Obama has gone."

"Oh, c'mon, Eleanor. Since you stay so involved with

what's going on, it doesn't look at all to me that your days are numbered. Anyway, I want to tell you this ugly story of mine. I'm not proud of it at all, but I need to get it off my mind." I rock back and forth in the chair, uncomfortable memories hanging in the air.

"Julie and Lance aren't your confessional pad anymore?" Eleanor looks at me with curiosity.

"No, not at this time. Because Julie was the recipient of a gift I gave her through the anonymity of the hospital where she went for treatment."

"Oh dear." Eleanor slowly gets up from the couch to look out the window. "Oh dear," she repeats again, looking at me, "go ahead with your tale of doom. This cold, cloudy day seems a perfect fit for it." She sinks back into the couch.

I continue. "You remember me telling you that I went to the Vermont Law School to study and practice environmental law. A subject very close to my heart... still is, in fact."

"Something everyone should be concerned about, especially with the Republicans and that crazy person running the government."

She's quite obviously perking up, and I'm reminded that it doesn't take much to pique Eleanor's interest, as long as she can hear you.

"When I got the necessary credentials to practice law in Vermont, I opened up a one-room office over an art supply store in Montpelier. At first, I was hardly making enough money to pay the rent, and black lawyers in Vermont were not exactly an everyday happening... or popular. But I put out some advertising on a local radio station, and slowly people began to come to me with all sorts of simple cases. I remember one about a trespassing herd of cows, one about a rabid dog who'd bitten several people, rent problems, accidents—pretty much all minor difficulties that could be settled easily. But it became enough to draw the attention of a group of people who wanted action on developers who were building houses higher and higher up on mountainsides, and going above legal height restrictions."

"I remember some of those arguments," says Eleanor, "when I ran The Pink Mallow Inn. I know I sided with those protesting folks." She's looking alert and interested.

"Yes!" Relieved that she seemed more like her old, feisty self, I continue. "So these people suggested I meet with them and go to the annual town meeting to get a sense of what was going on. There had been a general agreement on height restriction in the town, but it hadn't been enforced. Blakeville was a ski town with a well-known ski center, and rich people were arriving with glorified ideas of owning huge houses high up in the hills, like I said, above the already agreed-upon height restrictions. Money was the thing that allowed those in charge of building restrictions to look the other way. No penalty ever issued to any of those scofflaws. The town seethed with anger—some in defense, others in opposition."

"So how did you get involved with this nasty scene?"

"I totally agreed with those who wanted the restrictions to be enforced, and couldn't understand why everyone wasn't on board with them. After all, as I said in my speech that day at town meeting, a good part of Vermont's economic base is tourism. People come from all over the world to enjoy the pristine views, the freshness of the natural world, the plain beauty of the state. If all the mountainsides were covered with mansions and keep-out signs, Vermont would hardly be the same. And I could see that tourism would be no longer be an economic engine."

"You'd think people would get that...but I'll bet they didn't!" Eleanor snorts in derision.

"Oh, Eleanor, of course they didn't! Well, while I was working with this group, I saw some houses that defied description. One couple had built an enormous, sprawling house whose rooms, including the kitchen, living room, all the bedrooms and bathrooms, and so on, were laid out in a straight row, all of them with a fabulous view of the valley beneath. Anyone in a bedroom at the very end of the row had to track through the living room, three or four bedrooms and attached bathrooms to reach the one that was his or hers—crazy!

"But the weirdest thing in that house was the entryway, where there was a huge stone fireplace, nothing like anything I'd ever seen. Enormous boulders, all piled up in a heap and reaching the roof. I'll bet when they started a fire in that fireplace, until the fire got going and the stones warmed up, smoke was a nasty problem."

Eleanor is looking at me in amusement, and now she says, "Did you ever meet the owners?"

"No, I never did, but that wasn't all in this foyer. The owner had insisted on floor-to-ceiling supports in this cathedral-style room made from trees cut off his property. That was fine until the trees began to shrink, and soon they were dangling a foot or so from the floor. They had to be supported by big chunks of wood from a lumberyard eventually. It was a very strange-looking house!"

"Too bad you don't have a picture of this eccentricity," says Eleanor.

"I do have some somewhere," I say. "And others that we investigated. Like one huge place faced in white marble. It shone like a lighthouse on the hillside for miles. These people also put a Spanish-type red-tile roof on top of it. We all wondered how the Vermont winters would treat that extravagance until we were told they'd heated it underneath!"

"Well, now," says Eleanor, "none of this seems really scandalous to me, just stupid. People with money but no brains. Our USA really seems to be cultivating these types with a vengeance right now. But how did this involve you, Pat? Negatively, like you said in the beginning?"

"It was because Julie got sick," I reply. "Lance's landscape business had also fallen off—he felt it was caused by all these millionaires and billionaires coming into their town, which in turn gave rise to new landscapers with little or no training but who were cheaper than Lance, Lance who'd gone to university and had a degree in landscape design and maintenance."

"Julie was sick…how?" Eleanor looks at me seriously.

"It was cancer," I tell her. "Uterine variety. Their insurance wasn't going to cover all her necessary treatment, so this was where I made the judgment to help her."

"What did you do? You said yourself you didn't have that much money."

"Well…Eleanor, I took a bribe, something I now look back on with shame."

"What happened? Describe it to me." Eleanor looks sympathetic. Her glasses come off, she wipes them with a tissue.

"There was this one builder in the town," I say, "who had a shady reputation but was the darling of all the moneyed folk because he was able to get around restrictions. He'd even flaunted the law in places, like building houses on property that wasn't his and afterward denying that he had any knowledge of doing so. The case that involved me was one that involved the town's height restriction laws. He wanted to bypass these restrictions to build a huge development on a farmer's many mountainside acres of fields and woods. The real trouble here was incomplete knowledge of where this land ended. The old farmer didn't really know, although the land had been in his family for generations, and in fact no one really knew where the boundaries were. Boundaries have been a real estate difficulty in Vermont for centuries because the markers were things like 'the big beech tree' or 'the stone facing west,' very vague and indeterminate. When they sold their farms and woods, they never realized, I'm sure, that they'd be turned into private playgrounds for the super rich."

Eleanor sighs, "It happened around me, too, in our town. That was when I ran The Pink Mallow Inn. I remember the talk of some of my customers at the inn while their McMansions were being built up in the hills around us.... Anyway, go ahead Pat, this is really interesting."

"The case involved me and this one builder with the shady reputation. He'd bought this enormous property, he'd put in a road and he'd actually built a test house, without seeking much more than a permit to build. He'd proposed a very fancy, upscale development of houses that sold for a million or more on this land. My group discovered that this test house actually was built above the height restriction, and sued him. He was going to have to go to court."

"Ah," says Eleanor, "now I think I'm beginning to see your dilemma, Pat. So what was your next move?"

"So one evening this Burnham guy calls me and asks if I'd be interested in a proposal he could make me. I was surprised and insulted, really, that he would ask me, of all people, since I'd led the opposition to so much of this scofflaw stuff he was doing. So, quite firmly, I said 'no.'

"But he kept on talking as if he hadn't heard me. And then, so smoothly, 'but I heard your mother is quite sick and your parents are worried that they don't have the money for her treatment. Isn't that right? Miss Patricia McNally?'"

"I was astounded, Eleanor! How had he found this out? What nerve!

"And he continued with his non-stop talking, and over the next half-hour, I began to think how distressed I was after a recent visit with Julie and Lance, how awfully sick Julie looked and how upset she was by Lance's sadness and difficulty in admitting how little he could do to help her."

"That was innocent thinking. You only wanted to do

good. So what did you do?"

"It was suggested that I meet him for coffee in Burlington, where his office was, and listen to his proposal. Ten thousand dollars sounded awfully good to me, like a fortune really, and I reluctantly agreed."

"What was the outcome? Were you able to get this development through...or what?" Eleanor has now been sucked into my story. She leans her elbow on the couch and looks intently at me.

"The trouble he was having was the boundary line. And I was up against a pile of other problems: the neighbors who wanted nothing to do with a development of this magnitude, and my conservation group, who were all dead-set against any further construction—in fact, had ordered that the existing 'sample' house be pulled down. Did I already tell you that no house was going to be sold for less than a million dollars, which would completely change the heart and soul of that small town?"

"That was taking on a difficult load, Pat..."

"You can say that again. Anyway, I swallowed my pride and agreed to work for this sleazy character for the amount he and I had agreed upon. There was one redeeming feature to this awful choice I'd made."

"And what was that?"

"Looking for the boundaries of the property, high up on that beautiful hillside on warm September days, like the day we had out by your lake. I found a very old map that showed this family's property at that time, but the line was from a big yellow birch tree to an embedded stone facing west."

"Kind of like looking for the proverbial needle in the haystack," says Eleanor.

"Indeed it was. But walking up through that old pasture land was truly memorable. In fact, I still remember that part, it was like being out of this world."

"I suppose none of that is left anymore...am I right?"

"Unfortunately, you're right—it's all gone. Now it's all roads, houses, driveways, lawns, even a golf course. But back then I could see glimpses of blue, blue Lake Champlain in the far-off distance, like a ribbon threaded through this gorgeous palette of fall colors. Once or twice, huge flocks of geese would fly high above me, undulating, mystically changing their V formation, accompanied by honking chatter as leaders exchanged places. I met up with deer quite often, and once I frightened a bobcat who'd been sunning itself on a rocky outcropping. It streaked off into the woods when I approached. I saw a mama bear with her cubs ambling along the hillside, sniffing out berries and looking for nuts to fill their stomachs before their winter hibernation. I knew enough to stay well away from them, as there is nothing as protective and fierce as a mama bear with her cubs."

"Did you find anything that resembled a property marker?" Eleanor is always interested in details.

"Of course there were no yellow birches up there—they'd died or been cut down decades ago—but I did find the stone marker, and it was determined by the surveyors that the sample house, indeed, had been built well above the height restrictions. So we went to court, me to represent the builder, up against all the friends I'd made during the previous year there. I would have been with them, of course, had I not agreed to be counsel for the builder. I was a turncoat and got nasty letters from some of them. It was plain horrible."

"Well...did you win?"

"Eventually we did. I was able to persuade the judge that these homes were going to be environmentally friendly and would add favorably to the finances of the town, since most of them would probably be second homes and not require many town services, while paying high property taxes."

"So you got the money that was promised you?"

"Yes, Burnham was good to his word. And as soon as the case was settled, bulldozers came roaring in to plow up my mountainside heaven. Dust, dirt everywhere. My poor animal friends, I have no idea where they went or how they escaped this scene of total destruction. The whole thing was so demeaning, and I never went back to see. It was a horrible bargain, but Julie began to respond to her treatments, so at least I felt a bit better about it."

"I hope you can push all that away now," Eleanor says. "Remember that you had a compelling personal reason for doing so, Pat. I fully understand your move. Here, let me give you more tea." She tips the remains of the teapot into my cup and says, "And next time it will be my turn to tell you my Vermont story."

I'm relieved to get that part of my life out in the open. And to Eleanor, who is always so supportive of me.

Chapter 12

Eleanor

Today Pat is here in my apartment, again pestering me and anxious to hear the rest of my Vermont story. I begin.

"After my divorce and settlement—Tom and I had agreed to split the sale money of the house, which sold the day I put it on the market—I decided to do something entirely new. Rob was gone and Susie had started college, so why not?"

Pat nods and then says, "It's really kind of surprising, though...you always seemed so predictable."

"Well, I owned and ran the inn for twenty or so years. Now, Rob owns it, and he loves doing what I did... and runs the inn much better than I ever did, because I was an amateur...it cost me a lot of money over time. Eventually I did get it on a sound financial footing, partly because the Marlboro Music Festival started and we were inundated with guests from the Berkshires." Ah, yes, so long ago now, such busy days.

I say, "Susie went to college. I hired some extra help for the inn in the form of one wonderful woman, Ethel Hoyle, who could and did do almost everything for me."

Pat gets up off the couch and goes over to the house pictures on the wall. "Is this The Pink Mallow Inn? The small white house surrounded by apple trees?" She points at it and looks at me.

"Yes. But it wasn't as small as it looks in that photo."

"Nice photo though...did you take it?"

"No, one of my repeat customers. She came often and even set up and led a photography course for several summers up there."

"That must have helped your business. But tell me about your innkeeping, El. Was it fun or just awfully hard work?"

"It was both, Pat. When I first opened the inn, I truly thought I'd made a terrible mistake. I was always exhausted, some nights so tired I couldn't sleep. Remember, I'd only had a high school education, and that girls' school I'd gone to hadn't exactly prepared me for this kind of venture. Handle finances? Market a business? And as a wife in the 1950s, my husband had made almost all of the decisions, financial and otherwise. Oh! I remember when Tom saw me reading Betty Freidan's book, he grabbed it out of my hands and threw it into the fireplace, which was lit—we had a nice fire in that old house just about every cool evening...oh yes, some of those evenings, they were so nice..."

"That was quite a book," Pat says, interrupting my reverie. "It made a lot of changes in women's lives.

But...let's go back to The Pink Mallow Inn, El. What happened?"

"Well...to get a nice full breakfast ready every morning, I had to get up around four, and this after a long day of washing linens, cleaning rooms...I walked around like a zombie until Mrs. Hoyle entered my life."

"But you must have enjoyed meeting new people, didn't you?"

"At first, they all seemed like a blur in my mind. It wasn't until the repeats came back again and again, like the photographer I told you about."

"Did you ever have anyone strange, or a crook? Or did anything unusual happen? And tell me about Mrs. Hoyle."

"There were two things I remember so clearly." I am not about to tell her the third thing yet.

"We had a fire once, and do you know, what I still remember about that fire was the smell. The smell of burnt things, the smell of burnt things when water has been poured on them."

"A fire! That's awful! How did it start? Do you know?"

"I know only too well," I tell her. "When I bought the inn, there was a small apartment on the second floor, away from the guest rooms, over the big living room. That's where I lived. The living room was where people gathered and sat around, and I always had some coffee, tea and lemonade for them there—and when

Mrs. Hoyle came, she saw to it there'd also be a plate full of cookies or brownies, sweets anyhow, as she loved to bake. Anyway, it was a good thing, the fire chief told me, that my apartment wasn't over the kitchen, as the whole inn would have gone up in flames."

"Well, how did it start?"

I'm still embarrassed to tell this, after all these years. "I'd left the electric blanket on. It was an old one with no automatic shut-off and it just plain got too hot."

"Uh-oh! Did you lose a lot of things?"

"Yes, I did, actually. It was a terrifying afternoon. I'd gone out to the grocery store, no, it was Costco or one of those big places, for some staples. When I came back up the driveway and over the rise—the inn was on top of a steep hill—I saw fire engines, I saw firemen with long hoses, they were aiming water at the roof, where I could see smoke and flames. I got out of my car as fast as I could and tried to rush in and rescue my cats, but one of the men grabbed me and yelled at me to get back in my car and let them do the rescuing...their job, they said. So I sat and waited, frantic, wondering whether I'd lost everything..." I grew silent.

"Finish the story," says Pat.

"Dear Mrs. Hoyle had tried to be the savior. When she got there—her son, Roy, drove her to work every day—and let herself into the inn, she smelled smoke, and went all over the place to find out where it was coming from...and found my bed on fire. She tried putting it out by filling a wastepaper basket with water and throwing it on the bed, but it was of no use, so she called the fire department. Then she went outside and stayed outside until they came."

"What about your cats?" asks Pat. "And what did you actually lose?"

"My kitties were never found. I don't think they were burned, I think they probably ran away and found shelter someplace or with somebody else. My bed was burned up, I lost an antique chair, lots of family pictures, which I treasured, my carpet was ruined and I had to repair the roof. I was able to reopen in time for the summer season, and Susie came back on her summer vacation to help out, but that burnt smell remained, especially bad on rainy days."

"You were lucky, I guess," says Pat, "all things considered."

"Yes. After the fire mess was cleaned up, we had some very, very busy years. Susie had her wedding there. She'd met a very nice young man—who actually had been a guest—he was a teacher at a new school, in a town north of the inn, which had opened to help kids who were having trouble learning. It was a wonderful ceremony—even though Tom was unable to make it. He'd become confined to a wheelchair, and dementia had also set in."

Pat says, "I think I know that school. I was their legal counsel when they first opened. Appropriate, don't you think, since I had similar trouble."

"But the best thing that happened during those days," I continue, "was the day, the day that Rob walked in, totally unannounced."

"What! Your son Rob! The guy that might've been the one with us in the South? He didn't die, then?" Pat gets up and begins pacing around the room, she is quite the pacer when she's upset.

"Well, he was surely alive, alive as you and I are right now," I laugh. "But thin as a rail, and he had a beard and needed a shower, badly, as I remember."

Pat laughs, too. "How you remember smells, El! But tell me more, that must have been so exciting."

"Truly it was. And Rob was wonderful. He said he'd been teaching in a small rural school in the South, in Arkansas, under the sponsorship of the new governor and his wife, who'd done a lot for education in that state. Rob and his friends had managed to escape the drunks who'd beaten them up that night you told me about. And somehow they managed to get some food and water, and they survived their injuries, I don't know how. When they were feeling stronger, they managed to jump on a freight train, like hobos, and ended up in Arkansas. And since they all had college educations, they were able to find teaching jobs. Rob said the others had eventually found partners and decided to stay there, but he'd wanted to come home. I don't know why he never wrote to us. After two years, he went to our old house—in Newham—and learned where Susie and I were living...and so, turned up at our door."

"Wow," says Pat, "and where is he now?"

"As I told you, he still runs The Pink Mallow Inn. It's become a most desirable place to stay, with a fabulous restaurant, and he's thinking about a run for a statewide office there."

"This is such an incredible story," says Pat. "Wouldn't it be fun to go up there for a weekend, Eleanor? I could drive you. When spring finally comes, let's make a trip up there! And I'd love to see him."

"Pat! The final installment of my story is something that I'm not proud of. Just let me say it happened. When I saw that Rob could run the inn as well as or better than I could, I decided to take a vacation. I hadn't had one in years. So in April that year, I took myself off to Jamaica...and that's all I'm going to tell you for now, and it's your turn next anyway. And I have to go to dinner right now with Anna, so until next time..."

"That will be so very good. Now we're really learning important things about each other. Do you realize it's been almost a year since we met?" She puts on her spike heels and then her jacket. She gives me a big hug and disappears out the door.

Chapter 13

Pat

Today, Eleanor wants nothing more than a drive somewhere, maybe to see the Christmas lights that have gone up on people's houses, or lunch someplace, anything that's away from the complex. This is a lot easier than taking her shopping; she can be so slow now that she's behind a walker. I guess I'm an impatient person, really.

I fold up her contraption and put it in the trunk of my car. "Where to, Eleanor?"

"Pat. How about a trip out to your house today? You have some tea there, don't you? It's too early in the day for Christmas lights anyway—we can look for them on the way home."

Hmmm, I think to myself, she wants to stay out for some time; the complex must be getting on her nerves. I tell her I bought some of that Lapsang tea she favors, and we head out for my house.

"I love Christmastime," I say, "and my tree is up—it's a very pretty little one this year."

"Oh good! I wish my apartment had room for a real tree. But we aren't allowed to have Christmas trees, anyway." Her voice trails off, she must be thinking of times past again.

When we reach my house, I remove her walker from the car, help her up the few steps and go inside. The piney scent of my Christmas tree greets us.

"Oh, just like the Maine woods," says Eleanor, taking off her coat and pushing her walker into the living room, where she finds her usual armchair and sits down with a satisfied smile.

I'm in the kitchen, getting out the tea things when she asks me, "Pat, sometime I wish you would tell me about some of these fascinating objects you've got here. I bet there's a story behind each one. And...you've never told me how you got here, oh my, I bet that's a tale, too!"

I'm listening to her prattle on about this and that while I put the kettle on for tea and rummage around in the cupboard for the cookies she likes so much.

"Eleanor! I gave up law practice not long after that episode with Burnham. I was discouraged with the changes that were happening up there—money was paramount, conservation and the environment were having a hard time. Moreover, all of the friends I'd made and counted on there, had for dinner, and went skiing and biking with turned against me once they saw me take that case and win it. They'd hardly speak to me, they avoided me like the plague. This was very hard to take."

The water in the kettle is boiling, so I pour it into the teapot and let it steep. Then I put it on a tray and bring it over near Eleanor, pour a cup for her and a cup for me.

"I decided to go back to school, to go back into teaching, and applied to a Vermont teachers' college to brush up on new requirements for certification. I really enjoyed being back with kids in primary school, and at the same time I could enjoy Vermont winters. From time to time, I would strap on my cross-country skis and glide out on the trails all around my apartment. Cross-country was new for me, but I decided it was probably best not to break any bones on the slopes, and snowboarders who went too fast seemed to have taken them over anyway in places."

"That was a good move, I think," Eleanor says with a light smile.

"Yes. When I finally left Vermont and came here, I was given this little bronze replica of Rodin's 'The Thinker' by the parents of the kids I'd taught." I point out a statue that is in a special niche in my living room, and Eleanor rises carefully out of her chair to walk over and inspect it.

"What a thoughtful present," she says, looking at it attentively, and then laughing at her joke. "But you've done some traveling, too...look at all these wonderful molas and those strange carved animals. Are they African?"

"They are. I made a trip to that continent once, mostly to Kenya and Tanzania. I was with a group on safari. It's something I'll never ever forget. It was such a wonderful experience...the animals especially...but the scenery and the people, too. Those animals, I bought from an old whittler who'd set up his business by the side of a road. He was very proud of his work."

"As he should've been," says Eleanor, sitting back in her chair. "So, how did you get here—in this house, I mean. You still haven't told me."

"I moved near here because I applied for a job in a suburban school not far from here, a special school looking for an assistant principal, and got it."

"Weren't you the lucky one! Not many people can walk into something like that with so little experience."

"You've forgotten that my first job was teaching on that island, I'll bet."

"That's true," says Eleanor.

"Anyway, this school had been established by two formidable and wealthy sisters who wanted to help disadvantaged children. One of them, the older sister, had developed very painful arthritis and wanted to quit. So to make a long story short, I got the job of assistant principal.

"We worked hard at getting this school certified so that the kids could eventually transfer into regular public schools. I'm proud of the part I played in that school for so many years. Presently it's very well known for its enlightened erudition and its success in placement of students."

"I really like to hear stories like this, Pat. And what about this house? This very house of yours that we're in?" Eleanor's attention to details is still amazing, I'm thinking.

"I didn't have too much trouble finding it. It was small and in need of repairs, updating, but nothing I couldn't swing. And it had been on the market for several months."

"Weren't you the lucky one, again!"

"Yes, considering what's happened to the real estate market here since then. I hired a woman landscaper to make the garden you've admired and which, as I've mentioned, was my therapy for a long time. Still is."

"When I was your age at the Pink Mallow, that's what I liked to do best, too." Eleanor puts down her tea and says, "Pat, what an honorable life you've lived. You make me very proud to know you."

Most of the rest of the afternoon is spent telling her about my work and travels. At last, she gets up and pushes her walker towards the door, saying, "I think it's time for me to go home. What a nice day you've given me."

I take her coat out of the closet and start to help her on with it when she suddenly puts her arms around me, her head against my chest. "Pat," she says, "I love you so much. You've made my life bearable. I couldn't have continued on the way I was going for much longer. Thank you, thank you!" She gives me a big hug and I can see that her eyes are full of tears.

I'm left speechless. I help her into the car, stow her walker in the trunk and turn on the engine. What she said has touched me so deeply that I'm unable to say anything meaningful in return. So we ride back to the complex in silence...the Christmas lights in all of the houses beginning to light up the darkening evening.

Chapter 14

Eleanor

Since Pat has divulged most of her worst sins to me, I guess it's time to confess the next segment of my life to her. I'm talking to myself, standing in front of a mirror that is revealing an awful lot of my life...right here on my face.

However...Pat...she certainly seems to be a very accepting person of human fragilities...and seems to be able to move on without regrets. That's good. It's too bad more people aren't like her. I don't have too many regrets, except this one thing I'm about to tell her. I still wonder sometimes about that weakened moment of mine, which occurred so long ago. And what am I doing here? Have I lived too long? My kids are so far away and so busy with their own lives... so sometimes I wish...no! That's being stupid...never should wish that upon oneself. Oh good! Here comes Pat now! I can stop these depressing thoughts.

Pat sweeps in. She looks stunning. She's all dressed in chic black leather—boots, jacket—with a bright blue scarf around her neck. Right away, I feel better.

"Good morning, Pat," I say, as she gives me a hug, tosses her jacket on a chair and walks over to the window. "El, it's so cold out," she says. "I don't think we should go anywhere today."

"That's good. Because I've made up my mind to tell you about a piece of my life that I'm sure you would never think possible. I'm 'so predictable,' you know! But I hope you won't think I'm any a lesser person for what I'm about to tell you. I've never told anyone before, even Rob and Susie have no idea."

"I'm not the kind that makes judgments about people, although once that was something we were trained to look out for." She sits down in her favorite rocking chair. "Go ahead, Eleanor. Try me. You'll see."

I begin. "You remember Pat, about The Pink Mallow Inn?"

"How could I forget? It's not every day someone loses treasures through a fire and a missing son comes back to help his mother run an inn."

"Well, that wasn't all. When I went to Jamaica for a vacation...I fell for a most handsome black man."

"YOU! DID! WHAT!" Pat explodes. "This story of your life surprises me more and more," she adds. "Don't stop now. I certainly have to hear the rest of this."

I twist a bit in my chair to be able to look at her. "It's part of my life that I'm not exactly proud of, but it happened...and now in what I'm about to tell you, it seems as if it happened yesterday, and it's meant many sleepless nights for me."

"Go on." Pat eyes me intently with those green-brown eyes of hers. Back when she was a lawyer, she must have scared the daylights out of her antagonists with that look.

"I went to this lovely—and small and expensive—resort for ten days. It was managed by a Jamaican who'd been educated in England, at Oxford no less.

"I was picked up at the airport by a driver from the resort who told me all about him, his boss...how he'd come from a smart, hardworking family and had won a scholarship to Oxford."

"*Hmmm.* Sort of the same as me," Pat reflects.

"Yes," I say to her. "And sitting there in the car, coming in from the airport—I try to understand the driver's colorful language, hoping I can grasp some of the meaning...like when he told me, he no *winjy pyaa-pyaa*...he a real Ras." Pat laughs at my attempt to talk like a Jamaican.

"'What in the world is Ras?' I wondered...and when I met the man whom the driver had described, I instantly knew. This man was at the front desk when I walked in, and never in my life had I ever seen anyone handsomer. He was tall with unusual features. He had a long, aquiline nose and seductive brown eyes that immersed me immediately. His mouth was strong and sensuous. I was instantly captivated."

"Oh, God!" says Pat. "Then what?"

116

"He came from behind the desk and welcomed me in the most gracious way. His voice was soft and musical, but strong. He said he was glad I'd chosen his resort from so many others on the island, and he hoped I'd join him for dinner after resting a bit. He said that several other people were staying at Seasons in the Sun—that was the name of his place. He thought I'd enjoy meeting them, two English couples and an American couple on honeymoon who'd arrived yesterday from New York.

"Pat, he was so charming and attractive, in his presence then, I was absolute mush. Was I falling for him? Impossible, I thought. But had men been out of my life for so long, was I actually hungering for them, him...possibly? I was stymied, dreadfully puzzled by my thoughts as I followed a boy carrying my luggage to my private cabin."

"I don't see how you could have even thought you were in love so quickly! How long was your initial meeting—ten, fifteen minutes? How could you fall for a guy that quick? And a black man at that!" Pat scolds. "But go on. Sorry for the interruption."

"Well...the cabin was perched on a cliff overlooking a beautiful beach. Steps led from the patio to the beach, and after the boy left, I slipped off my shoes and stockings and walked down to the sand, feeling its warmth between my toes, and the warm Caribbean water sloshing over them. I walked some more on the beach, and the breeze made everything perfect. I returned to the cabin to unpack and rest before dinner at eight. In Vermont, I thought with some amusement, our dining room would be closing now and it would be bedtime for many of the guests. I assured myself, as I lay down, that this was going to be a perfect vacation."

"That certainly sounds great," says Pat. "Vermont winters are famously long, I well remember. But now you must finish your story, and I promise not to interrupt any more until you're done."

"OK. So before dinner that night, we all met in an airy living room for drinks. I only had one drink of an excellent French chardonnay, while the English drank something called Pimms, brownish-looking stuff. I was told it contained gin. We didn't stock it at The Pink Mallow Inn and no one had ever asked for it, so I was unfamiliar with it. My host, I noticed, held a glass of wine but rarely sipped from it. When the honeymooners arrived, we went in to dinner.

"My host—he told me his name was Desmond— was attentive and saw to it that I wanted nothing. Once he talked to the waiter...and Pat, I think I can remember some of what he said. It sounded like this: 'I man a tell you da lady have a *braata*, maybe she *manga gut*.' And then, his eyes twinkling, he leaned over me and said, 'I told the waiter to give you extra, as I'm sure you're hungry.'

"I laughed at him and agreed I was; it was the beginning of scanty rations on airplanes, and I hadn't eaten anything for hours. This first meal was delicious, and so different from New England fare. We started with a lightened version of *janga* soup, then a delicious shrimp dish with vegetables and ended with sweet potato pone, a kind of cake-like flan. Now, looking back on everything I ate on my vacation, I realize that I was introduced to many new tastes, like mombins and tamarinds, mangoes and papayas, guavas and yams, and bananas in all sorts of disguises. It was an eating adventure.

"That first evening was fun. The other guests went into shrieks of laughter when I told them about one incident at The Pink Mallow Inn when the Board of Health came to inspect my kitchen and marveled at its cleanliness when compared to others they had to inspect. What they didn't know was our fail-safe system of rodent-and-insect eradication—our two ferocious kitties were allowed to roam around there in the night and those unpleasant critters didn't have a chance."

Pat smiles, but doesn't interrupt.

"Dinner over, we assembled again in the living room for some strong Jamaican coffee, and shortly afterward, I excused myself and went back to the cabin to sit on the patio and listen to the night noises...the surf and the rustling of the sea-grape leaves. The moonlight danced on waves, and I liked the soft purring noise as the water moved on the sand. I wasn't particularly sleepy, whether it was the late-night nap or the strong coffee. Anyway, I didn't quite feel it was time to go to bed. This is heaven here, I was thinking, just plain heaven.

"Then I made out the figure of a man walking slowly along the edge of the sea towards my cabin. It was Desmond...I could tell by his gait and stature. I stood up and called out his name. 'Desmond,' I called. 'Mr. Rounseville...is that you?'

"'Yes, Ma'am,' his voice floated back up to me. 'I just wanted to make sure everything all right. You looked so tired when you came in the door this afternoon.'

"And he came up the steps. 'May I sit down with you a bit?' he asked, not quite sure, I think, of my response. I, of course, said yes, and that night we talked together for at least a couple of hours. The moon had nearly disappeared, and my watch said it was after two when I finally went to bed."

"What in the world did you talk about for so long?" Pat interrupts. "Sorry, Eleanor, but you know now how nosy I am!"

"Basically," I say, "I told him my story and he told me his—about how he was raised in a poor but ambitious family—especially his mother, who insisted her children, all eight of them, study their lessons with diligence so that they'd be able to go places. He had a sister who was a doctor in Haiti, a brother who was a lawyer in Kingston, and all the others were employed in one thing or another on the island. He was the only one, though, who'd managed matriculation at Oxford, and some of his family couldn't understand why he was wasting his education running a resort. But he'd employed many of them. The boy who carried my bags, for instance, was a nephew who was trying to make enough money to go to school somewhere in America. Anyway, he loved what he was doing and had met some famous and some equally infamous folk who'd walked through his door."

Pat, I can see, has become totally engrossed by my story. She's listening intently, her head supported by her hand.

"When we finally decided to call it a night, I thought he held my hand in his much longer than most people, and I didn't mind. It was warm and strong, and he smelled of the sea and the sand, and there was something about him that embodied all of Jamaica for me. And...that week, he proceeded to show me."

"Oh, Eleanor," says Pat, looking at me with trepidation. "This isn't looking good!"

I continued. "During those days, I'd be awakened at about nine by a uniformed maid—probably, she was another relative—knocking on my door and then coming silently in to leave a tray of breakfast treats, like a hot croissant wrapped in a napkin, and jam, fruit and juice and a large pot of that wonderful coffee. I'd put on my wrap and take the tray outside to eat on the patio, shooing away yellow birds that tried to steal morsels from my plate. The sun was wonderful, and when done, I'd put on my bathing suit and go out to swim, get some sun and walk for most of the morning, interrupted by some reading in a comfortable beach chair. Often the other guests would stroll by and we'd chat. Then it would be time for the buffet lunch at the main house. The afternoons were much the same for me, relaxing on the beach, napping—a real restful time. I didn't need anything more.

"At dinner, I was always seated next to Desmond, and he and I always found each other's conversation engrossing, stimulating and, at times, even seductive. He was a bright, pleasant man to be around, and I was falling in love, no doubt about it."

Pat groaned, but didn't say anything.

"One evening at dinner, he told us that a famous movie star was coming to the resort. He asked us not to do anything different from what we'd already been doing. The movie star wanted extreme privacy, and expected it.

"When she arrived, you should have seen the luggage! I realized that this star had seen her luster long gone, and to say she was a nuisance would be putting it mildly. Such demands! If she'd shown up at The Pink Mallow Inn, I think I would've told her to go and find another place. But Desmond was always polite and catered to her whims with patience, especially when it came to food—she would never eat what the rest of us were having, and his chef always had to prepare something different for her.

"In a whisper, just before I left for my cabin after dinner, Desmond told me he was going to dinner at a friend's resort the next night, and would I join him? 'That woman is driving me insane,' he said, 'what with her complaints about the food, the service, even all you good guests seem to annoy her. At least she's here only for two more days. Please, will you come?' And he took my hand again, giving it a gentle squeeze. So...how could I resist?"

Not a word from Pat. She is expressionless.

"Well, it was a wonderful evening. This place was high up in the hills, and the moonlight, the shadows from the trees, the sweet smell of the tropical flowers and fruits, it was almost overwhelming. We drank, we ate, we laughed at each other's jokes, and drove back to Seasons in hugely good spirits.

"'I can take Madame just fine now, El,' said Desmond, as he suddenly pulled me to him and gave me a kiss on the lips like nothing I'd ever had before.

"'You're going swimming with me tomorrow at a

place you won't believe,' he murmured, as he kissed me again. And I kissed him back."

"Eleanor!"

"Well, yes, Pat. And that night, I could hardly sleep, I was so in love with this man.

"And the place he took me to the next day was indeed a fairyland. A waterfall came splashing down over some mossy and fern-covered rocks to create a huge swimming pool surrounded by a tropical forest. Birds sang strange but lovely songs as we floated about nude—nude as the day we were born. I'd thrown all caution to the breezes and I didn't care, I was so, so in love. That night he took me dancing at another resort, it was equally romantic as the other one we'd gone to. We danced, he was a very good dancer, and with his arms around me, a hibiscus flower in my hair that he'd put there, I was in another heaven. Not surprisingly, afterwards we went to bed together and made the most passionate love."

"Good God!"

"He took me to the airport when it was time to leave with promises he'd come to Vermont when Seasons closed down for cleaning and minor repairs, which was also vacation for the help, and I came back to The Pink Mallow in high spirits. Even Rob said I looked twenty years younger. We had to gear up for the summer tourist season, and I worked tirelessly, but wondered unceasingly why I hadn't heard anything from Desmond. I lost many nights of sleep thinking about him, just like any lovesick teenager. Then, right around the Fourth of July, to my surprise and unmitigated horror, I realized I'd been seduced—and was pregnant."

"El! Eleanor!" Pat grabs my arm, "Are you OK? You seem to have drifted off just now..."

I guess I must have gasped or made a funny noise, as the look on Pat's face is one of consternation. "I'm fine, Pat, really."

"What did you do?" Pat's voice is barely a whisper. "Did you get an abortion?"

"No. No abortion. When I realized I might be beginning to show my condition, I made all sorts of comments to Rob, Mrs. Hoyle and the rest of the staff about how fat I was getting. I bought some voluminous clothing to hide being pregnant. I found a wonderful, caring place in Burlington for unwed mothers and went there for regular checkups. I stayed amazingly healthy and thought no one at the inn ever suspected my real troubles. When it was time to deliver, I told them I was going away for the weekend—to a conference in Burlington and then to visit some friends up there. Rob didn't suspect a thing, but I think old Mrs. Hoyle may have been suspicious...although she never said a thing to me, even when I returned."

"I don't understand why you didn't have an abortion the minute you found out you were pregnant!" Pat gets up and starts to pace. "I did. Remember?"

"Yes. I remember your story," I say. "But then, I'm a generation older than you. My life was somewhat stable. And I couldn't do it. I believe all women have the right to choose, but I am of another generation... and I'm the old-fashioned type—I grew up when such things were never discussed and women like me didn't really think of themselves as having many choices in life. I went ahead with the birth. It wasn't easy; I was in a good deal of pain, as the baby took its time coming into the world. When it did arrive, it was healthy, the nurses assured me. Before I delivered, I'd said I didn't want to know anything about the baby, whether it was a boy or a girl even. 'Just put it up for adoption, and I'll never, never inquire who it went to.' I didn't want to know anything about it, ever. And they agreed to honor my wishes."

"This all seems so unlike you," Pat says, still pacing. But smiling. At least that look of alarm has disappeared. "I'm having a hard time getting all this in. But I'm so glad you told me, since you know so much about my imperfections and me. Maybe it's time to talk more about our other transgressions..."

"Yes, Pat. But not tonight. I'm too tired to talk more. I'd like to eat my dinner and then go to bed. Funny, how all this reminiscence has exhausted me. Please, please save your criticisms for next time."

Pat looks at me strangely, puts on her coat and leaves my apartment without a word more.

Chapter 15

Eleanor and Pat

Eleanor, talking to herself: Oh damn! The telephone! Who on earth can it be at this late hour! My bed's been calling me to come in and stretch out and snuggle down under the covers.

"Hello?" I answer the phone in a peevish sort of way. *It's Pat! But Pat doesn't sound like herself. Her breathing is audible. Her voice is intense and I can tell something has upset her.*

Pat: "Eleanor! I have some very bad news to tell you. I have to go to Vermont…Julie and Lance are dead."

Eleanor: "Oh my God, Pat, what happened? Of course you must go, but tell me, what happened?"

Pat: "All I know, Eleanor, is from my friend Cindy, a nurse in the hospital up there. She was working the ER this evening when they were brought in…an auto accident…they think caused by poor visibility…it's snowing up there."

Eleanor, interrupting: "That's so strange, Pat. Weren't they used to driving in snow? They were old-time Vermonters, for heaven's sake."

Pat: "Indeed they were. However, this past summer,

I talked with Lance and suggested that maybe it was time for him to forget about driving at night. Both of them are getting on...but obviously he didn't hear me or chose to ignore my warning."

Eleanor: "Oh dear, another case of elderly stubbornness."

Pat: "Yes. And particularly after having a few beers. Apparently they'd been to some kind of holiday party, celebrating the New Year and that Julie was completely free of cancer."

Eleanor: "I'm so sorry, Pat. Of course you must go. I need nothing tomorrow...and I wish you safe travels— and *the best of love* to you. What a horrible shock."

Pat: "It is. It's a terrible shock! Somehow, I thought those two would live forever. Anyway, I'll come right over when I return. Take care of yourself, Eleanor, I can't lose you, too!" She hangs up.

Eleanor: My Pat doesn't deserve this. Those two people up there in the Kingdom must have been wonderful people— the sort of people sadly missing in this world. Imagine! Adopting a black baby, probably amongst all sorts of critical neighbors. I wonder how many of my generation would take that on. Anna, for instance. Hah! Not many others either, I'd guess. I wish I'd met them...Pat was going to take me to Vermont this summer and I would have met them for sure... but now it's too late...how sad this is for us all. I think I'll make a cup of chamomile tea, it helps me think clearly and sleep better...and then I'll go to bed.

* * *

Pat: It was over a month before I saw Eleanor again. I did talk with her on the phone, telling her about the service I arranged for my Julie and Lance...so many friends in attendance...the myriads of legal matters and paperwork... good thing I'd been a lawyer.

But I didn't tell her about the stunning discovery. It blew me away when I read it. In fact, I just about passed out. Good thing there was a chair nearby to catch me.

I had to tell her face to face, there was no other way. I bought a huge bunch of white roses, her favorite flowers, to bring with me when I came. I did tell her, though, to be prepared for important news. But I refused to divulge what it was over the phone in spite of her pleas. Believe me, it was hard for me to resist.

When I reached Eleanor's apartment, I could hear voices within and realized she and that tiresome old friend of hers, Anna, were having quite the conversation. I stood in the doorway, wondering whether I should go in all the way.

I heard Anna say, with some heat in her raspy voice, "El! Ah'm so glad yuh've stopped seeing so much of that black girl. It's nice tuh have yuh back in the bridge game again."

Then I heard Eleanor reply, ever so softly, "Yes, I suppose I did spend a lot of time with Pat..." But her voice was very low, she seemed unsure.

Anna croaked, "Well, then! Ah'm glad yuh've seen the light! What made you think you two could evah be such close friends?"

"Anna, Pat is a good friend of mine, she always will be. We've talked our lives over, we're like sisters...but really more like mother and very able daughter, since she's so much younger than me."

Anna banged her cane on the floor. "Now, don't you be talking like that! Y'all know better than tuh say that. Just plain disgustin'! Disgraceful!" Bang! bang! went her cane again.

"Well, maybe..." Eleanor was vague. "You know, I haven't seen Pat in some time. She had to go north, but she's back now. She called today and said to be prepared for some big news." She continued in this tentative, unsure voice.

"Just so's yuh don't see her so much, it's unhealthy!"

At this, I decided to enter. After all, Eleanor was now much more than just a good friend to me.

"Hello, Eleanor! Hello, Mrs. Eastman!" I was cheerful, kind of fake-breezy. "Whoo! It's surely a cold day out...it looks like we might get some snow." I was staying on the positive side, even though Anna's glare felt like a laser burn.

"Oh, Pat!" said Eleanor warmly, coming toward me with outstretched arms to give me a hug. "I'm so glad to see you!" I handed her the roses. "Ooh, how beautiful," she said. "I was hoping..."

And suddenly, without any warning, she crumpled to

131

the floor. Anna and I stared at each other in horror. I tried to pick Eleanor up and help her into a chair, but she had no response. I felt for her pulse and there was none. Eleanor had died.

Anna screamed at me, shouting, "Look what you did, black girl! You killed my best friend! You are evil! Evil! Ah'm callin' the poh-lice on you!" and she stomped out past me without even looking at Eleanor. She slammed the door behind her.

I was mute, stunned by Eleanor's lifeless body. Then, reaching into my purse for my phone, I dialed 911.

* * *

In going through Lance and Julie's papers, I was astounded to come across a birth certificate from Burlington, enclosed in a letter from the place Eleanor had told me she'd given birth. It stated quite clearly—there it was in official print—that Eleanor Riley had delivered a baby girl, a negro in fact, and the father was a Desmond Rounseville from Jamaica. This proved, without a doubt, that Eleanor and I were mother and daughter...just the way she had stated to Anna only yesterday. I don't think Julie and Lance ever knew this, and now...and now...I am the only one who knows.

As I write up notes for the eulogy I must deliver tomorrow at Eleanor's funeral service, I debate whether I should reveal this astonishing information, the news that

I was prepared to tell Eleanor the day she died. It goes and forth in my head a thousand times. But in the end, I realize that I'm still the only one who knows, and for now, maybe it's best to keep it that way.

Other Stories

Caveat: *Adde Parvum Parvo Magnus Acervus Erit*

"Beware: Add a little to a little and there will be a lot"

There is a small island off the coast of Maine where members of a big family from mostly the Boston area return Capistrano-like every summer. In this big family are two little girls, ages nine and ten, who have decided that this summer they need money. They have devised, after much thought, an enterprising scheme by which to do so. The penny candy counter at Crockett's store, in the village, presided over by patient Miss Lucy, was just too enticing to pass by every time Mom or Dad took them to town.

"Do you think," says Jane, the ten-year-old, to her cousin Emily, who is nine, "that they would let us use a rowboat every day?"

"Well, why not?" says Emily. "We wouldn't ruin it—at least I don't see how we could, even though garbage is not exactly the cleanest stuff in the world. We could ask that they put it in proper bags."

Seems younger Emily is more assured than her cousin about this scheme. "And besides, we will be occupied. They always say to us to get busy, or get outside and do something—we'd sure be doing something then, wouldn't we? Right?"

"Okay," says Jane. "But I think we should test out our idea before we really go into business. Like who will row the boat, who will talk to the customers, who will pick up and carry the garbage, and what should we charge."

So the girls go down to the dock where the rowboats are tied and choose the biggest one to get into. "We'll have lots of room for the trash if we do this," they agree. Struggling with the heavy oars and trying to set the huge old rowboat on course is a challenge. It soon appears that neither girl is big enough to row the boat alone, so they sit together on one thwart and each pick up an oar.

"When Dad took me to Harvard once," says Jane, "We saw the Harvard rowing crew on the Charles River. It looked to me that there were separate people rowing together to a kind of song. They count *one-two-one-two* in a kind of rhythm. It was neat."

"So we should try that," says Emily. "Let's just go up the creek first to see if we can."

"*One-two, one-two*," they sing in unison, but somehow the girls don't quite get the smoothness of the Harvard crew. Jane is the stronger of the two and manages to pull the boat around in circles as Emily, valiant to the end, pulls hard on her oar but not quite hard enough to keep the boat in a straight line. There's also a lot of splashing and "catching crabs," which means the oars are slipping out of the oarlocks and becoming useless to the rower.

"Well," says Jane, exasperated, "Emily, I don't think you really know how to row. Let me show you how it's done." She fits the oar back in the oarlock and pulls hard, but catches a crab in spite of her best efforts and falls backward off the thwart.

Emily can't resist a giggle. "So, smarty," she says, pursing her lips at Jane, "is that really the way?"

Jane's face is red with embarrassment. "No. Of course it isn't, dummy. I'll show you how, just watch." She pulls herself back on the thwart and fits the oar back in place and starts to row. "You see, you have to be smooth to do it; now it's your turn."

Emily sets her face in a determined grimace, assured that she can row as well as her cousin. With practice she proves that she can, she is a strong little girl. After several days, they form quite a good rowing team, both seated on the same thwart and pulling equally, almost, at the oars. They row up the creek and down, singing over and over *one-two-one-two* as the oars are dipped and pulled out of the water.

At the big old summer house, no grownup is aware of what these two are doing. To their parents, the girls seem to be busy and happy, so no questions are asked. As the summer progresses, the harbor begins to fill with all manner of pleasure craft, and the girls eye them with anticipation while they stand on the dock surveying the scene.

"I think we are ready," says Emily to Jane, "I think I can row almost as good as you, and look, there are three sailboats in the creek this afternoon. It is getting late, so I bet they'll stay overnight."

Jane looks out at the boats and says, "Okay. Tomorrow before breakfast, let's get in our boat and go and collect their trash and garbage before they leave for someplace else. We agreed on a dollar a bag and then we each get fifty cents."

Now this price may seem to some a rather big expense for garbage removal, as in the old days when one went cruising, the detritus was simply dumped overboard into the sea. No longer is this possible—boats now have to have "heads" (that is the nautical term for toilets), which are contained on the boat, and therefore sailing folk have problems in disposal of garbage, trash and sewage. And there is a heavy fine if one is caught doing the illegal dumping. (But it is all for the good of cleaning up the ocean around us.)

The girls were quick to realize their business opportunity. The next morning they make ready for their first customers by getting out of bed early before any of their parents are up and silently creep their way down to the dock. They get in the big rowboat, unhook it from the dock, settle themselves on the thwart, and start rowing out to the first sailboat in the creek. A man is up on deck and notices the girls as they row closer. "Well, good morning, girls," he says, "What gets you out so early?"

There is some whispered conversation between Jane and Emily as to who should answer this cheery greeting.

Jane takes the lead. "Yes, sir," she says. "Do you have any trash or garbage you would like to get rid of?"

The man looks at them and smiles. Then he puts his head down the companionway, and the girls hear him ask, "Hey, honey, I have two business ladies topside. They will remove any garbage or trash for us. Send it up." Then he addresses the girls. "How much do you charge for this service?"

"It's a dollar a bag, sir," says Emily, now picturing many afternoons peering over the candy counter at the store.

"That's fine," says the man, handing them a dollar bill and also a large trash bag almost full. "Good luck in your enterprise. I think you have a very good idea."

The girls thank him and row away to the next boat, but no one is on deck.

"They must still be asleep," says Jane. "Let's try the one farther up the creek and then come back to this one. Maybe they will have woken up by then."

So they turn the boat up the creek and see that on the next boat there is a woman on deck with a dog, a little black one, that starts barking furiously as they approach.

"What on earth do you girls want?" says this woman. Her voice is nasal and she sounds cross and tired. "I see you pestering that other fella." The little dog at her side growls and shows his teeth.

"We wonder if you would like us to take away your trash or garbage," says Emily, just a bit startled at the woman's tone.

"I don't have any," says the woman, "so go away and don't bother me again."

The girls stare at her in wonder. They have never before met rudeness. "We were just trying to help," says Emily, in dismay.

"Don't need no help," she replies, "so GO AWAY!"

"So sorry to bother you," adds Jane. "We will not disturb you again." And the girls row back to the dock, rather unsettled by the woman and her nasty little dog.

"Should we try that last boat?" Jane wonders.

"Yes. But I'm hungry," says Emily. "Let's do it after breakfast."

Breakfast over, the girls slip away again to try the last boat anchored there in the creek. They row out towards the boat and find, to their delight, three big boys sitting on deck drinking coffee.

One of them notices the pair. "Hey," he calls out, "what are you two up to this morning?" His other two friends give amused looks at the girls but don't say anything.

"Well..." Jane is hesitant, the boys look very messy to her, sleepy-eyed and disheveled. Anyway, she continues, "We were wondering if you have any garbage or trash that you would like to get rid of?"

"Oh, my," says the boy who spoke first, "do we ever!" And he slides down the companion way and starts handing up six-packs of beer, one after the other, at least ten cartons. Then up comes a big bag of trash. The boys hand over the stuff and the girls are in a quandary as to what to charge for all the old beer bottles. "I think," says Emily, making a quick calculation, "we will have to charge you twenty-five cents for each cardboard box of bottles, plus a dollar for that bag of trash."

"So that's your little business." The first boy seems

to be the only one who talks. "You little ladies are going places. I bet in a few years I will see your names as heads of major corporations listed on the stock market." He laughs, "C'mon guys, pony up. We need to pay these ladies their wages. I figure we owe them three-fifty."

Full of cheer and laughing, the boys search their pants pockets for change and hand over just the correct amount to Jane and Emily, who now have four dollars and fifty cents for the next trip to the village. They row back to the dock in a state of bliss.

"Weren't they nice boys," says Jane, as they stowed the trash and bottles as best they could under thwarts in the rowboat.

"Yes," says Emily, "but don't you think they drank an awful lot of beer—and this garbage bag is full of not much more than empty chips bags. My mother would be horrified."

"Mine, too," says Jane.

In the following few days, the girls collect quite a nice sum of money, but the trash in the rowboat is also beginning to pile up. They had not thought out how they were going to dispose of all this when the boat really could hold no more. But that day had not yet arrived. So they begin to scout out boats in the harbor. They are becoming very sure of themselves and enjoy meeting the sailors on the sailboats especially. These people appreciate the girls' service and once or twice they receive extra money. Their trash collections and money pile up and they never had any more dealings with anyone like the nasty woman, until...

One day, a huge motor yacht comes into the harbor. On board there is a crew, all dressed in white uniforms scuttling about, setting anchor and doing all the necessary operations to stay the night. This yacht has tinted windows so the girls can't see much else besides the white-clad crew.

"Wow!" says Emily, jumping up and down, "this should be a fortune for us! Should we go over now or later?" She looks at Jane, who is just standing and staring at the huge yacht.

"I don't know, Em," says Jane. "I've never seen anything so big come into this harbor. First of all, would they be able to hear us if we came over and asked for their trash? That boat is so darn big. And I bet they have air conditioning and stuff like that with motors running."

"Oh, so what. Just think of all the trash they must have on that thing." Emily starts to get in the rowboat and Jane, somewhat reluctant, follows her.

They row out into the harbor, even if the old rowboat now is stuffed with trash and garbage, and beginning to be quite rank. They circle the huge yacht, where at last one white-clad sailor notices them. "You girls can't come on board, you know," he yells at them, "if this is the reason you keep rowing around us. This is Frank Sinatra's boat, but he is not on board."

The girls look up at the sailor. Emily is the first to speak. "That's okay, sir. All we wanted to know was whether you would like us to remove your trash, if you have any. It's a dollar a bag." And then she turns to Jane and says, "Who's Frank Sinatra anyway?"

"Oh, he's an old-time singer, Emily. My dad and mom like him—they have a record of him singing, and sometimes I've seen them dancing together to his singing."

"Oh, well, here it comes," says Emily, while the sailor on board Frank Sinatra's boat hands over an enormous, heavy bag of trash that almost sinks the old rowboat. A dollar bill is sent down in an envelope. The water is up to the old boat's gunnels. Several sailors now are up on deck and are looking down at the girls. "Hope you make it back to shore," one of them teases.

"Whoever Frank Sinatra is," says Emily, "he hasn't taught his crew much. I thought crew people were polite. At least all the others we've met were." She sticks her tongue out at the sailors. "So much for you boys," she says, also raising her hand in an impolite gesture.

"Listen Emily," says Jane, "don't be rocking this boat so much, we have to get back to the dock without sinking, you see how close the water is, don't you? And anyway, who taught you how to do that? That's really rude, you know."

"My brother taught me," says Emily, "I know it's rude but they deserved it, handing us this huge bag. We should have charged them more."

"Just pay attention until we get back to the dock. We have to hope that no one comes by in a speedy motor boat or we surely will sink." Jane is concentrating on her rowing and looking out for any problem boats that might tip them over with their wake. The wind has come up and rowing this overloaded boat is tricky as the waves splash against the sides and a little water pours in each time.

But the girls make it back to the dock. However, to their surprise, on the dock are their fathers, standing and waiting for them.

Jane's dad is flinty and not smiling. He is a writer and has been busy writing a third novel and playing golf or tennis in his time off. He and his wife and Emily's parents have not been down to the dock for those weeks while the girls have been about their business. It's still quite early in the summer and the sun has not yet taken enough chill off Maine's icy water for the parents to swim.

"We thought you could get the truck and help us take all this stuff to the dump," says Emily, bright-faced. She's got that candy counter perusal securely fixed in her mind.

"You did, did you?" says Emily's dad, smiling. "Well, we will help you do that, but first you will have to take it all over to the boathouse where the truck is parked and load it up. Then we will drive you to the dump."

The girls devise a system for unloading all that stuff that was beginning to smell awful, like true garbage. Emily, at first, stands on the dock while Jane is in the rowboat handing her bag after bag. Then they switch, and after two hours of sweaty work, manage to get all the bags into the dump truck, a good way from the dock. They struggle through scratchy bushes, wrestling with loads that seem to weigh more and more as they stagger along on a rocky pathway.

"I sure hope all this work will be worth it," says exhausted Jane to equally exhausted Emily, who collapses on the steps of the boathouse.

"Well, look in the bag and count up the money," pants Emily. "I bet we have at least ten dollars."

Jane sits down beside her and opens the bag. Sure enough, inside she can see all the dollar bills they've collected like treasure. "I count exactly ten dollars," says she. "Now we must tell them to get us to the dump. Quickly, before the store closes."

Emily and Jane have kindly fathers, who, having watched the girls struggle with this trash and load it into the truck, agree to take them to the dump, where they will have to negotiate with the dump master.

He's an old Mainer type and looks serious as the girls start to heave the bags of trash into a huge container that will be hauled to the mainland and its contents buried somewhere.

"Girls," he says to them, "you kinda got a lot of stuff there. It'll cost you ten dollars to get rid of it all."

"Ten dollars?" both Emily and Jane cry together. "But that is all we have." And their sad little faces fall as sweet thoughts of Crockett's candy counter evaporate like fog sometimes does along the Maine coast.

"Ayuh," says the dump master, nodding, "that'll be what it costs ya."

Angst

Fog, pushed by fickle southeast winds, rolls in and out of the harbor at Summer Island. To Caroline, slowly walking up the long dirt driveway to the main road, it bears little resemblance to the line in Carl Sandburg's poem about fog. *There's no little cat feet about this*, she thinks, as she brushes water droplets off her old sweater.

She walks on steadily. Today she's decided that she's too fat, hence her decision to take a long walk even though rain was predicted. She has walked up this driveway many times, as she used to come to the island every summer with her parents during her childhood, and made many friends here over the years. She thinks of them as "summer" friends because most of them live far from her home in a Boston suburb. She has always envied the sophistication and extreme good looks of the girls from New York or Philadelphia, girls who have all of the teenage boys spellbound. Caroline doesn't have anyone after her like that, but she has admired one boy particularly. Unfortunately, she has admired him from afar, as he's never said much more to her than a breezy, "Oh, hello Caroline."

His name is Ted, and he is a very good-looking blond boy who can sail circles around all of the other boys in the Summer Island community, who always wins all of the tennis matches and who can hold knowledgeable conversations on current events. She has often heard him and admired his intellect, as his parents and hers are friendly and have dinner together frequently. He is one of the most popular young people in town, even among boys his own age.

Looking out at the harbor as she walks along, she notes that for a Labor Day weekend not many pleasure boats are anchored. *I wonder if this has anything to do with the war talk I hear just about everywhere*, she says to herself.

Spruce and fir trees are the silent witnesses to her footsteps. She stumbles over a big stone, then stops to pick it up and throw it into a lush growth of ferns bordering the driveway. She stops at a culvert under the driveway and notices the small puddles nearby. She picks up a small stone and aims it at one of the puddles, but misses—it rolls off into a pile of similar stones.

Can't even do that, she laments, as if someone were there to hear her complaint.

The main road shows up at last, with big streamers of fog playing against one another. Caroline watches them from the top of the hill, at the end of the driveway. Mournful foghorns groan in the distance, sometimes punctuated by toots and whistles of boats traveling through the passage between Summer Island and its bigger island neighbor. *It's funny how fog accentuates all noises. Even my footsteps crunching gravel are audible. Never noticed that on sunny days,* she thinks.

Should I go right or left? If I go left, I'm headed to that small community of artists, sculptors and writers who stay in modest cottages around a rock-filled harbor that's daunting to even the most practiced navigator. These people, Caroline knows, keep mostly to themselves. They aren't sailboat racing types, are never at the teas held at the little yacht club on Saturdays after the races are over. But they take all of the prizes at the art show at the library, held every year on the next to last weekend before Labor Day. Caroline goes every year and admires the display of so many images of Summer Island. Her dad has repeatedly said, "Look at how many ways people can show just rocks, water and trees."

Caroline decides to head for the harbor, a more familiar area. It is a more heavily populated area, and it's where the lobster fishermen work. It has a public dock, so cruisers can land and walk to the grocery store. Her summer friends tie up their rowboats or little sailing dinghies there sometimes. She thinks, *Maybe I'll get a chance to see Ted. He might be sailing his dinghy out in the harbor, practicing maneuvers to play on competitors when racing in the Saturday races. Or he might not be sailing. He might be home this ugly day, reading some serious book in an effort to hold his own during cocktail discussions. Or he could be playing tennis with friends. It isn't raining that hard, so it is really quite possible that this is where he'd be.*

Caroline trudges along. She puts her hand up to feel her hair—it is another horrible problem, as dampness makes her hair into masses of ringlets all over her head. She tries patting it down into something more manageable. *Oh, it would be just my luck*, she thinks, *to have Ted come along now with my ugly hair, my dirty old sweater and my fat self.*

Nearing the harbor, she hears the engines of the lobstermen's boats, either going out to set traps or coming back with their catch. She hears them conversing now, as she hears herself still crunching gravel at the side of the road. One car passes her, and it is nice old Mrs. Parker, who stops and asks if she wants a ride. Caroline shakes her head, saying she's too fat and needs the exercise. Mrs. Parker laughs and says, "Caroline, you don't look fat at all—but have a good walk anyway." She rolls up her car window and drives away, disappearing around the bend.

I'll go as far as the harbor, Caroline says to herself. *Then I'll look to see if Ted has taken his boat from the dock and I'll know if he's out in the harbor.* She trudges steadily onward. One car passes her and then another, the harbor is almost in view. A third car comes from behind her and sounds its horn. Caroline jumps aside, nearly losing her balance. It is Ted and he is driving this car. Another young man sits next to him in the passenger seat.

Ted has slowed down to match Caroline's pace. He rolls down the window and, sticking his head out, says to Caroline, "Hey girl! What're you doing so far from your house? You want a ride? We can take you there."

Caroline is nearly speechless. Finally, overcoming being addressed by this very special person, she stammers, "N-n-no. I'm just fine, I'm taking a walk."

"Oh, c'mon! Get in—you're getting soaked! Really, we can take you home, we'd like to."

Caroline stammers again. "N-n-o, I really want to walk home. But thank you."

"OK then. Have it your way, but don't say I never asked you!" He rolls up his window and revs up the engine, and soon he, too, disappears around the bend.

Caroline stops walking for a moment, disgusted. *What were you thinking? You had a chance to be with him and yet you turned him down. What an idiot!* She shakes her fist into the air and stamps her feet as if she was marching. *Now, without a doubt, I'll never have that chance again—what a dummy!*

And with these sullen thoughts, she turns around and makes her way homeward.

*　*　*

The summer has ended and soon it is time to go back to school. Caroline is a high school junior, and at times wonders quite a bit about her future, what with this horrible war looming. Every bit of news is discouraging...her friend's older brothers drafted into the Army or the Navy...it is all strange and upsetting.

One day, on returning from school, Caroline finds on the front hall table an envelope addressed to her in a heavy scrawl. The envelope is thick, expensive. She opens it and searches the enclosed notepaper for the writer's identity. At the bottom of the page, she finds the signature. It is from Ted, now a senior at a boarding school.

Caroline sits down to read the letter with shaking hands.

"Dear Caroline," it begins. Caroline looks at those two words repeatedly and then reads the rest of the letter, amazed at its contents.

Dear Caroline,

I am writing to you to ask you a favor. You seem to

be a person who knows her own mind and can make decisions. I am planning to enlist in the Navy. This is very upsetting to my parents as they were counting on me to go to Harvard—you know I was accepted, don't you.

But I want to help in our country's war effort and so I have enlisted in the Navy. What do you think? Would you be so kind and write me your thoughts and suggestions how to appease my parents?

Sincerely,
Ted

Caroline reads and re-reads every word again and again, sitting there in the dark hallway. The words mesmerize her, she can almost feel Ted's hands as he steadied the paper and wrote them.

In the evening she writes her reply. This is what she writes.

Dear Ted,

So nice to hear from you. Of course I think you should enlist. I think you should do what YOU want to do. It's your life after all. Make your parents see that. You can go to Harvard later.

Sincerely,
Caroline

*   *   *

Caroline never receives another letter from Ted. She hears from a friend that he had indeed joined the Navy. A year later, the same friend tells her that he is missing in action and presumed killed. His submarine was the target of an enemy torpedo somewhere in the Pacific. No one on board escaped alive.

For a while, she harbors guilty thoughts about urging him to enlist, but then she hears that before going overseas he shacked up with a beautiful, exceptionally bright, artistically talented, superb tennis player and formidable sailboat racer—one of those unattainable girls from New York or Philadelphia, and romantic and guilty thoughts about Ted mostly diminish. She now thinks about him only occasionally, as one of those summer things once alive in the past.

Daylight Saving Time

Mabel and Al are retired. For many years Mabel worked as a secretary-receptionist at a plumbing supply company where she met Al, who was a plumber and a pretty good one at that. In Oldtown, Al occasionally moonlights a plumbing job or two now and then, but keeps it down so that he doesn't screw up his taxes.

Mabel is delighted at last to be in her home all day and says to Al, "Oh, my, Al! This life of luxury is just too much...I hardly can get used to it."

She settles herself down in a chair facing Al at the small table where right now they are enjoying a leisurely Sunday breakfast in the breakfast nook. Mabel, a heavy-set woman, has even put up the wallpaper herself, which she thought very tastefully designed with smiley-faced teapots, cups and saucers surrounded by twining vines.

Mabel still has on her bathrobe and Al is dressed in khaki pants, white socks and black shoes, but still in his undershirt with no sleeves.

Mabel says, "You know, Al, I think last night was daylight saving time."

"Yeah, I know," says Al, not looking up from the newspaper, "I think I saw that."

"What is it," asks Mabel, "do we set the clocks backwards or forwards? I always forget."

"Seems like it should be backward," says Al. "We get more daylight then, stretched out kinda, wouldn't you say?" He is still reading the sports pages while Mabel gets up and wanders around, looking confused.

"Oh, I'm not so sure." Mabel sits down again and looks into the depths of her coffee cup as if she could find the answer there. "Seems to me, there was a saying to make it easier to remember, like spring forward or fall back...or was it spring back and fall forward? Huh? Whaddya think it was, Al?"

"I dunno, Mabel," replies Al. "Maybe I can find it someplace in the paper." He remains absorbed in what he's reading.

But then, as if he had a second thought, he continues. "Seems to me that you'd fall forward, face down like, if you was attacked."

"What's attacked got to do with it?" asks Mabel.

"Nuthin. Except like showing what seems normal

if you was attacked," answers Al, looking up from the newspaper.

"Well...the clocks won't set themselves. We gotta do one or the other, backwards or forwards it has to be. Jeez, I wish I could remember." She pushes her coffee cup aside and gets up to stare out the window.

"I dunno. But I say we set them backward. We lose an hour," says Al, "but that's OK. The day will be longer then." He holds out his arms, showing how the day will be stretched.

"OK," says Mabel, "you're usually right, Al. It's just about nine so I'm going to set this clock back an hour." She bustles over to the stove and sets that one back.

"You're so right, Al, it does seem like daylight is now being saved. There now, this one is fixed, we just have to remember we did it already. You go fix the grandfather in the hall, but with care, Albert. Remember it belonged to my grandmother."

"Don't I always," mumbles Al, his mouth full of glazed doughnut from the local Dunkin' Donuts store that he always buys on Saturday for their Sunday breakfast.

So, in this household, this Sunday in March, all the clocks were set backwards. And Sundays, most always, were set aside for their daughter Marcia and son-in-law Kit and their twins to come to lunch. But this morning Mabel takes it easy, saying to herself, "Oh, good—I have plenty of time before they come."

"Let me have the women's pages, Al," she says, pouring herself another cup of coffee and heading into the living room to read the gossip of Oldtown on the La-Z-Boy.

A little later the doorbell rings. Al gets up to answer it. Passing Mabel he says, "Jeez, I wonder who that is so early?"

He opens the door and there in front of him are his daughter Marcia, husband Kit and the twins.

"Happy Daylight Saving Day, Dad," says Marcia, with a big grin on her face.

"What the heck time is it, for Pete's sake," says Al, holding on to the front door as if it were a life raft.

"Just about twelve noon," says Marcia. "What time did you think it was?"

Mabel, from behind the newspaper, isn't fazed. "We'll just have to go out to Sevior's," says she. "What a difference time changing makes! I get all confused for at least a week, until I get used to it. You all come in and watch the TV and I'll run right up and get some proper going-out clothes on. Won't be a minute. Help yourselves to coffee. There's still some left in the pot, I think."

She goes upstairs to dress while Al, Marcia and the twins gather in the kitchen to wait for her and discuss the rigors of daylight saving time, and son-in-law Kit adjusts all the clocks in the house to *two* hours ahead.

Technology

Gina and Rose are having coffee together at the Main Street Café. Now it's an almost every morning ritual since they retired. Gina had been a dental hygienist and Rose had been an assistant librarian in Oldtown. They met at the town's senior center a while ago, but decided that the coffee at the café was a whole lot better and the pastries there were also fresher than at the senior center. So, at least two or three times a week they get together and discuss their retired husbands or their children who have flown the coop.

Gina pours herself a cup of coffee from an alignment of Green Mountain coffee jugs placed on a large table in the café where everyone is to help themselves after obtaining a cup from the clerk at the checkout desk. She decides on Breakfast Blend and laces it liberally with sugar and light cream. She holds a paper plate with a rich, gooey Danish pastry in her other hand and walks over to the table where Rose sits.

Gina says, "Rose, aren't you having coffee this morning?" She sets her cup and pastry down on the table and sits facing Rose.

Rose says, "Gina. I'm just so discouraged with myself. I cannot, for the life of me, make my computer work. I sat up last night until two in the morning, trying to get beyond what it said was 'log in.'"

"You have a computer now, too?" Gina looks at her friend in amazement. "You told me, after hearing me complain so long about mine, that you never wanted one. You said the telephone was just fine."

"Well, yes, that's true, Gina; but yesterday my son Al came by with his old Mac and told me it was time I learned how to work a computer. He set it all up for me and said I was ready to go online. And then he showed me how, but he went so fast that the notes I took down I did not understand. Oh, Gina, I'm so discouraged...I feel like such an idiot..." Rose buries her face in her hands.

"Now, Rose, don't be like that," says Gina. "I'll get your coffee. Same as usual?" Rose looks up and nods without much enthusiasm.

Gina gets slowly to her feet and walks over to the clerk to buy one for Rose. She pours coffee into it from one of the jugs with the same generous amounts of sugar and cream.

"Well, I have a Dell," says Gina, handing Rose her coffee. That's a P.C., which a Mac is not." She sits down, with a little smirky smile.

"Anyway Rose, tell me why you stayed up 'til two a.m.?"

"I was trying to get online," says Rose, "and my notes said to Google it. Now what in the world does that mean?"

"First, you have to turn on your computer. Did you do that?"

"I think so, all these little pictures appeared on the screen's left side."

"Did you put in your username and password?"

But Rose only says, "Huh? I think Al did that for me. He said I was all ready to go online. He picked out 'Rosypetals,' sort of like my name, as my password but I didn't know where to put it and to tell the truth, I couldn't remember my username either."

Gina sighs. "Well, if you could remember those things, you should have been able to log right in. What IS on your desktop?"

"My desktop? Gee whiz, Gina, the computer takes up all that space now."

"No, Rose, I don't mean *that* desk top. The screen on your computer is called a desktop."

"Oh, yes, I forgot. Go on, Gina, what else could I

have done wrong?"

"Those little pictures you saw on the desktop are called icons," says Gina, "I must say though, I always thought icons were church related, but now there's another meaning for the word—just like 'gay'."

"Do you think," asks Rose, sipping her coffee, holding the cup with both hands, "that maybe the world has passed us by—a bit? Because I remember your troubles, Gina, when you first got your Dell."

Gina laughs, "Don't you remember, Rose, me telling you about the time I went to print something and the machine wouldn't stop, no matter what I did—until it ran out of paper."

"Kind of a waste of paper, wasn't it?" says the ever-practical Rose, "and from what I've heard we are wasting more paper than we ever did. And another thing, my mouse doesn't always work on the icons, as you call them."

"Sometimes you have to click once, sometimes you have to click twice on them. You find out which ones by doing."

"But where do I want to go?" Rose is still confused, her eyes fill with tears.

"You want to go to the menu page to figure where you want to go."

"Is that where the Internet is? I wanted so much to get on the Internet and email my kids in Texas." Rose's eyes are full with tears. "I spent hours looking for a picture—no, I mean icon—that said 'internet'."

"It doesn't say internet, Rose," Gina instructs, "but you have to be connected to a network."

"Al said I was connected." Rose's tears drip softly on the table.

"Well, then, you should just put your mouse on I.E., which stands for 'Internet Explorer' and then you type in 'www.google' and there you are, able to get Gmail."

"Gmail?" says Rose, "I want to do email." And tears keep rolling down her face.

"You put an address before the words 'Gmail' just like the post office, only no stamps. Your address will be 'Rosypetals' just like you told me." Gina truly is trying to help her friend, she hands her a Kleenex.

"Oh, my," says Rose, "then what is 'aol.com'? That is on my Mac somewhere, as I saw it once, I think. But when I tried to send an email to Mary in Texas, I'm sure she was waiting for it, it wouldn't go. It kept asking for the password and then some funny, squiggly numbers and letters showed up asking me to copy them. I did, over and over. And still nothing happened. It was then almost two a.m."

Gina nods, so wise is she. "Yah, well, that happens. It happened to me a lot when I was learning."

"And then, would you believe? A whole lot of advertisements came on the screen...and then, Gina, you wouldn't believe what next showed up." Rose gulps her coffee. Her tears have stopped.

"So...what showed up?"

"A whole lot of pictures of men and women," Rose is whispering now, "and they didn't have any clothes on. And do you know what—they—were—*doing*? Oh, my, Gina! I will never, ever tell you what I saw!"

Joe

This story is about Joe, and also about my best friend, Carol. Carol was a teacher, an artist and a poet. She was and still is unconventional in the best sense of the word. Carol was also married. It was not the happiest of marriages, as her husband was high up in finance, wore suits and loved boats, in that order. I never saw much affection between them, although they did produce three outstanding children.

Carol and I are now in our eighties and still meet occasionally for a drink or coffee, whichever mood we find ourselves in. One day, when we both had lots of time, she told me a story about her neighbors in Vermont.

Years ago, she had purchased a hippy handmade house in the mountains. It was her defense against vacations forever on the sea, an unpleasant scenario, as she was prone to horrible seasickness. She had shown me pictures of this unusual house, mostly built of scrounged lumber, bargained-for stained glass windows, water from a spring, and questionable electricity. Truly it was a house of the 1960s, and one in which I saw Carol happy with her paints, and with notebook always ready for a creative project.

Carol's memories of this place are so clear, I'm sure she still misses it a lot, as well as neighbor Joe, who this story is really about.

That afternoon, Carol told me, "I can still see Joe, down on his knees, grubbing away, happy in his garden, tending to his precious plants—fantastic dahlias and cannas, and enormous quantities of green beans, squash and tomatoes. His old red pickup truck parked nearby, as it stood always ready for a run to the village in case his wife, Janey, needed something from the store. Sometimes it was also heaped high with fragrant fertilizer that Joe had negotiated for from some local dairy farmer."

Carol first met Joe one morning when she had gone up to Vermont alone for a weekend. She was sitting outside the front door on a rickety, splintery old bench that the previous owners had somehow forgotten, enjoying the warm spring sunshine and a cup of freshly brewed coffee. An annoying peewee's chirping somewhere up under an eave suddenly gave way to the noise of a rattling, banging engine coming up the driveway.

Soon an old red pickup truck came in sight, drove right up and parked not far from her. She stood up, briefly wondering at this bold action and whether she should be afraid. Maybe this person had a gun? However, when she saw a bent-over older man crawling out of this truck and hobbling over to where she stood, her uncertainty turned into mere curiosity.

Here's how she told me the story:

"My name's Joe," he said. "YOU sure don't look like the kind that was here before." He let fly some spittle, as if he were chewing on tobacco, and then pulled out a cigarette from a battered pack and offered me one, which I declined, having given up smoking.

"Where do you live?" I asked him. I was still wondering about this odd, but seemingly friendly character dressed in layers of old clothes that, from even a short distance, emanated a strange smell of sweat, garden dirt and old tobacco, a weathered and lined face not often bothered by a razor, and this weird unattractive habit of spitting as he talked.

"Me and the wife live down below." Spit. "She's kind'a frail, had a cardinal arrest lately, so she's gotta take it easy fer awhile." Spit.

"Oh, you're my nearest neighbor. Is that your house,

the one I pass just before I turn into my road?"

"You got that right." Spit. "Say, what did you tell me your name was? And did you tell me where you was from?" Spit.

And he pulled another cigarette out from the packet after grinding out the former one, only half smoked, under his well-worn boot heel.

"You intend to live here?" Voice is definitely puzzled, punctuated by more spit.

I told him my name was Carol, and said, "No, I won't be living here. I bought this place for holidays. My kids and I love to ski. We live in Massachusetts. I could only afford this place in this town—it's expensive here. But it's an alternative to always going on vacation on my husband's boat."

"Your husband a Navy man?" Joe looked at me, his thick eyebrows raised. "I'm a retired Merchant Mariner myself. Been all over the world. What's wrong with you? Boats, as you call 'em, best way to see the world!" Spit. Then he continued, "Massatoosits, you say? My Janey's from Massatoosits." Spit. "She sez Vermont's better."

I stood up to say goodbye, and before I could get in a word of thanks for his visit, he'd turned towards his truck and was giving me a Navy-like salute, saying, "I'll be goin' now. I'll tell 'em you look OK, so's if you need anythin' jus' holler." And after that brief inspection, he climbed back into his truck and rattled off down the driveway. And that was the beginning of this thirty-year friendship.

As she tells me about Joe, I can see that Carol is there in Vermont. There's a faraway look on her face when she describes how every summer weekend that she was there, mysterious bags of just-picked vegetables could be found outside the front door. Or sometimes it was a huge bouquet of dahlias, cosmos or another kind of summer flowers, or a pie or cake or cookies.

"Joe was very good at fixing things," she says, "from frozen pipes to extracting cars from snowbanks, and was always refusing payment for a job well done. I must have asked them a thousand times to have dinner with me at home or in a local restaurant, but they always declined."

"Do you still keep in contact with those two?" I ask.

"We sent Christmas cards to each other for a long while. Then theirs stopped coming to me. I found out Joe had died. And Janey, sadly, well, I have no idea what happened to Janey. I can only hope she's in a safe place with caring people, just like they were to me."

What's in a Name?

At the Sunnyside Retirement Home, Charley (known as Chuck) and Charlotte (known as Lotte) are now good friends. Lotte is a widow and Chuck's wife ran away with another man many years ago. Both are in their mid-eighties, and now keeping fit is one of their goals, so most days they go to the gym or fitness center, as they don't like group exercise classes.

Before Lotte and Chuck were acquainted, one day, as Chuck was pounding his size 14 Nikes down on the treadmill, he caught sight of Lotte trying to get on a nearby stationary bicycle.

"Hey lady," he called out in a friendly manner, "you're new here, aren't you? I'm Charley, but most people call me Chuck. Might I be so bold as to ask your name?"

Struggling to get up on the bike, Lotte answered

him. "I suppose you could call me new here, although I've been here six months. And yes, my name is Charlotte, but most people I know call me Lotte."

"It's funny that I've never seen you around," said Chuck, still carrying on his workout, although now puffing heavily, "and I don't ever recall seeing you at dinner."

Lotte, finally up on the bike, started to pedal. "Well, I've mostly had dinner in my apartment. I tried going into the dining room by myself, but no one sat with me and I felt as if I was Exhibit A with so many pairs of eyes upon me. But I often go into the sandwich shop for lunch. I've met some very nice people there, but I don't recall *ever* seeing you there." And she gave him a small, sly smile.

"Well! We'll fix that situation right away! How about joining me and some friends for dinner tonight, and we'll all try to cure your lonesomeness." Chuck got off the treadmill and stood in front of Lotte, who was still pedaling away on the bike. He was smiling to himself, as if he had found something new and very desirable.

"That would be very nice," said Lotte, and she gave him a broader smile this time. "Is there any special time you'd like me to come?"

They agreed on a time. That evening led to many other pleasant evenings. They found mutual friends, they told each other about their families and former lives, and about their likes and dislikes as well. In fact, they became very companionable.

One evening Chuck asked Lotte a strange question. "Lotte, what do you think about all those dating sites you find on the computer? You have a computer, don't you? Have you ever seen those dating sites, especially the ones for people over fifty? Revolting, I say!" A look on his face expressed disgust.

"Yes, I have a computer, Chuck. I suppose those dating sites are all right for some. I had a friend who met a very nice man that way and they're still together, I'm told. But it isn't for me. I'd be scared to get myself out there like some women do."

"It's certainly not for me either," said Chuck, "There are too many predatory females out there looking for rich husbands. I won't go near any of them, and they're all over those sites."

"That doesn't mean, Chuck, that there aren't a large number of men out there who're looking for a nurse or a purse—I've got no interest in them either! After being married to a holy terror, raising my four kids, being a counselor at a children's hospital and doing all sorts of volunteer work, I'll be damned if I'll take on any sloppy old men...oh sorry, Chuck. This doesn't apply to you, but I hope you know what I mean."

"Yeah, I guess I know what you mean. When Louise asked for a divorce, I gave it to her pronto. I'm through with lazy, complaining women! You don't know they're that way until they've snuck into you, and you end up marrying them and then...better watch your wallet."

They pushed their chairs away from the table, stood up, said goodnight all around. Then Chuck and Lotte proceeded to their separate apartments and eagerly turned on their computers to find the dating site, "Just for Seniors," where they looked for their electronic friends and possible romantic attachments.

On this computer site, Lotte was known as Diamond Lil and Chuck's name was ChuckWhoSees. They were ever hopeful that they'd attract serious partners. ChuckWhoSees had posted a picture of himself when he was much younger; he is dressed in a dark suit and striped tie as if he were the CEO of something important. At Sunnyside, he had grown a beard and his eyebrows were down over his eyes, looking like prone bottle brushes.

Diamond Lil never put her picture up on the site, but was thinking of doing so when and if she lost some weight. Knowing that some men preferred older women, she had described herself as witty, charming and rather seductive, hoping to catch the eye of some male who appreciated those traits.

Hope springs eternal, it is said. And finally a female connected with ChuckWhoSees. He was totally smitten. His lover boy efforts went something like this:

TAP, TAP, TAP.

"So...Diamond Lil. How are you doing tonight?" SEND

And she replied.

TAP, TAP, TAP.

"Just fine, ChuckWhoSees. And by the way, I think we know each other well enough now for me to say to you I really don't like your handle. It sounds too childish. Couldn't you think up something more adult?" SEND

TAP, TAP, TAP.

"Diamond Lil! What do you think people will get from that name? Sounds like you've been out gold digging! If you're looking for a rich husband, sure ain't gonna be me!" SEND

TAP, TAP, TAP.

"If I was, I surely wouldn't be admitting it online!" A little unvoiced giggle. SEND

TAP, TAP, TAP.

"Good! I'm glad you clarified that. Might I be so bold as to inquire...just where do you live?" SEND

TAP, TAP, TAP.

"I just moved here about six months ago." SEND

TAP, TAP, TAP.

"That's funny, so have I...but about two years ago. What street are you on?" SEND

TAP, TAP, TAP.

"I believe it is Church Street." SEND

TAP, TAP, TAP.

"That's also funny! That's where I am too! How about we meet for coffee tomorrow at Sevior's Café around ten?" SEND

TAP, TAP, TAP.

"I would be delighted. But it will have to be a quick one, as I go to a gym at eleven." SEND

TAP, TAP, TAP.

"That's great! I also go to a gym about that time. For identification, I will wear my old captain's hat with gold braid for Diamond Lil." SEND

At the appointed hour, Chuck, aka ChuckWhoSees eagerly awaited Charlotte, aka Diamond Lil, inside the café. Indeed, he was wearing his old captain's hat but he'd perched it on his head at a rakish tilt, deciding this gave him an air of certain youthful insouciance for this important meeting.

Meanwhile, Diamond Lil had spent a good bit of time assessing which outfit she should wear for this important event. She decided on a black suit with the idea that black might make her look trimmer than she actually was. She arrived at the café a bit late, and there sat her old pal Chuck, wearing a tired old captain's hat for sure. They both stared at each other in horrified silence and then broke into hearty laughter.

Chuck said finally, "For Pete's sake, Lotte, you're as

big a liar as I am."

And the very cool Lotte answered, "Well, Chuck... like they say, it takes one to know one! And what time do you want to eat dinner tonight?"

One Day at the Pumping Station

"Well! I'll be damned! I knew those boys awhile back!" Joe tosses the *Boston Globe* on the floor. He gets up from a once fine armchair, which serves as the only comfort at Oldtown's water department's pumping station. None of the men who work for the department mind its broken springs, torn upholstery and sprouting stuffing. It's a place to sit and the only one, rescued awhile back from the nearby dump, or—in deference to all the newcomers who've moved to Oldtown—the "transfer station."

Joe is in charge, mostly, of fixing things that break, whether it's the water department's pumps or other machinery, or systems belonging to in-town customers of Oldtown who rely on paid-for, properly functioning water and sewage systems. Joe doesn't deal with the outlying residents who have to rely on their own wells and septics, as Oldtown's water and sewage system does not go out far. After all, Oldtown is a small town.

Joe is happy in his job for the most part. He was recruited from being head foreman on a nearby farm where the boys grew up, the boys whom he has just read about in the newspaper. It was a nice job then, but with his own growing family, Joe felt that the water department job guaranteed health insurance and a few other perks that the farm owners could not do, no matter how nice they were. The boys were something, though, and had worked with Joe, as he did farm chores for a long time until they went away to college. And now— Joe picks up the paper again to assure himself that he really sees what they were doing. "I ain't surprised," he says to no one in particular. "They was quite a pair."

As he sits down to thoroughly read the *Globe* article, he notices the boys' picture and admires their looks. He reads on. It seems they had started a whisky-making distillery, first experimenting in the basement of the old farmhouse where they had lived. They admitted to fooling with making hard cider at college (no surprise there, his own son had done that), but these boys went on with their booze business until they had perfected the ultimate bourbon whisky and now were making a bit of a fortune for themselves. Rare, as New England is not noted for its whisky-making capabilities.

Joe gets up from the chair and stares out the window. The nearby pond has frozen over in the night. "Jeez, even those damned geese have gone; it looks as if winter is really comin' on." He settles himself back in the chair and gloomily reviews his thoughts. And then to himself, he says, "I wonder if *I* could do it?"

"Do what?" a little voice in Joe's head asks him.

"Naw…" Joe gets up from the chair and upsets a big empty can that someone meant to throw away at the Transfer Station.

"But there sure ain't much goin' on around here." Joe paces back and forth in front of the window where he can see the frozen pond. "Well, a coupla more hours, then time to call it quits. Maybe tonight it will get real cold and I'll hafta deal with a frozen pipe or two an' water floodin' all over folks' basements."

Joe sighs and sits back down in the chair. "At least that's sumpthin' to do."

The telephone rings in his pocket. It's Mrs. Platt, Joe's wife. "Honey," she says, "I'm all out of bird food, it's gettin' cold and my birds are hungry. Wouldja stop at Agway and pick me up a bag on your way home?"

Mrs. Platt is an active birder and the Platts have bird feeders in every corner of their yard.

"Sure thing," says Joe, "Will you need anything

else?"

"No," she says. "Anything happening down there?"

"Not a thing, it's been a right borin' day." He checks the gauges, sees that all the lights are glowing on the big tanks, the pumps are working, everything is properly humming away, and decides to call it a day.

Joe stops at Agway on the way home and wanders among the assorted bags and bins of birdseed. He buys black sunflower seeds for the birds and a bag of cracked corn to keep the squirrels away from the feeders and heads home. Mrs. Platt is glad to see him and gives him a big hug as he steps in the door.

"Fill the feeders, wouldja?" she asks. "And oh, I'm glad to see you bought some corn. Them dratted squirrels been at the feeders all day, scarin' off the birds."

Joe takes the bags of seed and corn, fills the feeders and starts to strew the corn around under them, muttering, "Sure is getting cold." The wind is icy and smells of snow.

At dinner, Joe says, "I read today in the *Globe* 'bout the Baxter twins. Remember them, Rosie, at the farm?"

"Sure," she says, "Why were they in the *Globe*, for goodness sake?"

"They are makin' whisky somewhere and makin' a lot of money at it."

"*Hmph!*" Rosie puts down her fork. "What with all their educatin' that's a funny way to make a livin'.

Wonder what their folks say about that!"

"Well, I ain't gonna call them up and find out, but I think it kinda clever."

"*Hmph!*" Rosie gets up and starts to clear the table. Joe retreats to the living room and puts on the television but somehow cannot find anything of interest. Football season is over, his Patriots went down to defeat and baseball hasn't begun. Hockey and basketball are of no particular interest to him.

And then—that astounding late afternoon idea overcomes him. "What if *I* made whiskey myself?" he says to himself. "I sure could do it right down there at the pumpin' station and no one the wiser. There's all the stuff there I need. Just got to make the mash first, I guess. Wonder if there's any of that corn left in the bag I bought. It'd be right nice to sit down with Rosie one night and have a little *smooooth* somethin' before dinner like the fancy folks do."

Thinking about how he would go about this task, he remembers from high school science class that in order to distill anything, one has to create a vapor first, which means heating the mash.

"Hey, dear," Joe yells at Rosie, still in the kitchen, "What happened to that big old beat-up pressure cooker we had?"

"Out in the shed. That's where I last seen it, I think. Why you want that old thing?"

"Nuthin' in particular. I was just thinkin' about sumpthin'. Like maybe I should start to clear out all the junk we've got stored out there."

"Now, that's a real good idea, Joe, since I've been after you for years to get rid of some of that stuff!"

Joe goes out to the shed and sure enough, there's the old pressure cooker up on one of the top shelves.

"Perfect," he thinks. "Now I hope I left some corn to make the mash."

There is about a pound of corn left in the bottom of the five-pound bag. He puts all his necessary treasures in his truck and the next day heads on down to the pumping station.

Much to his surprise and dismay, since he isn't sure this kind of activity he has planned would be sanctioned by the powers of Oldtown, he sees that his friend Eddie has opened up before him. Eddie is a retired fireman and often helps any of the Oldtown's municipal workers when he gets bored and wife Sal tells him to get out of the house. Eddie is a good worker and can turn his hand to most anything that is a problem. Eddie has been given a key to the pumping station's door just in case of any emergency.

Joe walks in with the bag of corn and Eddie immediately asks, "What's with the bag, Joe? Didja bring lunch for me, too?"

"Mornin', Eddie. Nope, this ain't lunch." And then,

to his surprise, blurts out to Eddie, "I'm gonna try and make me some whisky. Real, *smooth* Kentucky bourbon whisky. And I think I can make it right here at the station. We got all the stuff to do it with, *right here*." And he shakes the bag of corn in demonstration.

"Gawd, Joe! What made you decide to do that? But hey, that's a good one, if you ask me. A little snort of it before I go home would make it *smoooother*, like you say, between me and that sometimes old battle axe."

Joe laughs, "Aw Eddie, Sal ain't no battle axe. She just tryin' to keep you on the straight and narrow. Anyway, what we got to do first is wet this stuff and let it get into mash. I read that it takes a few weeks to do, so we got time to plan our action and keep it away from any that comes nosin' around."

"Well. All's I want to know's why you can't just go up to the likker store and buy a bottle so's ya don't hafta go through all this trouble?" Eddie is puzzled. "Yer Rosie ain't like my Sal and a'gnst drink, is she?"

"No, she ain't. But if I get seen by some higher-up like that town manager jerk Tom or one or two of those selectmen, walkin' into the likker store and comin' out with a package from there, I could be the talk of the town. Ya know how this here Oldtown works."

"Awww," Eddie says, "Well, let's see. Whaddya do first?"

The two men wet the corn in the bag and set it away

in the dark behind one of the huge water tanks where no one would likely go.

*   *   *

After about two weeks' time Joe says, "I think it's time, Eddie, to see about the mash."

The corn has sprouted little humps and bumps. "That's disgustin' lookin'," says Eddie. "Now whaddya do?"

"You rub off all this stuff," replies Joe, "and then pound it into mash. Then I'll put it in this old pressure cooker here and set it on the burner and get it up to boilin'. You, Eddie, get that long piece of copper pipe over there and we'll twist it into shape to catch the vapors into this here jar. That's the distillin' piece. Long and curly does the trick. So now, go and twist the thing around this old can, it'll be just what we need."

Joe points at the old neglected can and continues to pound the corn into a fine mash. Eddie, meanwhile, fights with trying to curl up the recalcitrant piece of copper pipe, twisting it this way and that around the can and when done, stands back to admire his efforts.

"Gawd, Joe," he says, "this here is a work of art. But don't ask me to get in such a wrestlin' match agin."

Joe nods approvingly. "That's real good work, Eddie."

When Joe finishes pounding, he puts the mash, adding a little water to it, into the bottom of the big old pressure cooker and sets it on the gas flame usually used for soldering broken pieces of pipe together. Then he goes about pumping station business as Eddie stands at the door acting as lookout. When the mash has heated to about the right temperature they guess, they strain it through a kitchen strainer that Joe has also found in the shed, and add yeast that he had taken from Rosie's immaculate refrigerator. Rosie was slow to get up, so she never saw this pilfering action.

"When that thing on the top starts to jiggle," says Joe, pointing again at the pressure cooker, "that's enough heat and we gotta take it off and let it cool for a day."

The telephone rings at the pumping station. Joe answers and says to Eddie, "That's old Mrs. Flagg. She's got water runnin' down into her basement from somewhere, she says. Whaddya say, Eddie, we go and see what's the trouble, fix it and then grab some lunch at Sevior's Café."

"OK with me," answers Eddie. They set the pressure cooker to cool, get in the truck and head on downtown.

*　*　*

For several weeks now in Oldtown, Tom, the town manager and Mary, his girlfriend, have been watching the actions of the water department personnel at the pumping station as they come and go. They park their car, along with several others, at the head of the long road that leads, eventually, to the pumping station. This road is very popular with walkers who go with their kids or dogs along the many trails on the conservation land that surrounds the pumping station.

But Tom and Mary do not take walks there. Instead, once they've seen the employees leave, they walk into the pumping station building. (Tom, being town manager, has keys to all Oldtown's official buildings.) Tom and Mary have had several assignations on the old easy chair there in the empty office, no one the wiser. Today, they can hardly wait. Mary strips off most of her clothes and throws them on the floor. Tom unzips his pants, his fingers fumbling in anticipation, and they go at it with gusto.

The door opens and Joe and Eddie walk in on them.

"My God!" says Joe, his finger pointing at Tom, "and YOU a married family man!" The two men stand in front of this disheveled pair, not really knowing what more to do or say.

Then a fearful explosion from the room where the mash is cooling—a frightening sound of crashing metal pieces splintering and landing on the floor or bouncing off walls—pierces the pregnant silence of the four.

Then soft plopping sounds—*splat, splat, splat*—as if they were all in a huge, loose-bowelled bovine barn.

"NOW! What the hell was that?!" Tom demands,

in his best, quickly-put-together authoritative town manager's voice. He's had trouble in zipping *up* his pants and stares at Joe.

Joe stares back. "Only my efforts at whisky making," he replies softly and sadly. But then he brightens, as he says, "I really got'cha, Tom, this time. But you can bet, I won't tell on you if you won't tell on me."

Eddie stands mute, his mouth open in an O, his hands folded across his stomach, while the girlfriend, curled up, is sniffling and shivering like some wounded animal on the old chair.

"Agreed," says Tom, the town manager, offering Joe his hand.

Antarctica

This little cruise ship is headed from Chile's Punta Arenas to the Antarctic Peninsula; in their tiny stateroom, Brenda is trying to stuff her now-empty suitcase under the bunk, without much luck. She gives the bag another kick, sits with a thump on top of the bunk and says to her husband, face flushed with exertion, "I dunno, George, about this cruise. Seems to me, livin' in New England like we do, goin' to see more ice and snow's really dumb—like I told ya, I'd a lot rather be in Vegas."

"It's been the dream of my life, Brenda. Y'know that. Ever since Admiral Byrd comes into the garage and tells me all about it."

"Yeah, and you believed all that stuff coming out of such an old man." Brenda is still kicking at her bag under the bunk. She gives the suitcase an extra-hard kick.

George gets up from a chair where he has been fiddling with a locked bag. "It was just my luck that their car got a flat tire in front of my Dad's garage...or we wouldn't be here, at all!"

"You were just a kid then, George. Funny that you could remember all that stuff they told you."

Brenda stands up and looks gloomily out the porthole, seeing little else but water. "And another thing, George! With all that money you won in the lottery, seems to me we could'a had better accommodations on this here ship. Where we are, I bet they call it steerage. I wish we were back in that fancy hotel in Santiago.... Now, *there's* a place I could'a spent my whole vacation time...not bothering with any old ship headed for ice and snow."

"Well, I did tell ya, ya didn't need ta come—but just think, Brenda, what we're gonna to see! We don't have anything like them icebergs or penguins in Oldtown. This is 'n adventure! I'll feel just like old Byrd or one of them polar explorers. And look...." George has finally managed to unlock his bag. "I've got this new camera." He carefully pulls a gleaming Nikon from its case and beams at her, showing his new treasure.

"And just how much did'ja spend on that thing?" Brenda goes over to inspect it, her head going up and down like an angry bobblehead doll.

"Prob'ly about as much as you've spent on all them new clothes," says George. "And yeah, it wasn't cheap, but I wanted the best. I figure I ain't comin' back this way very soon, if ever. *So why not!* And, besides, the guys at the club want me to give them a show when I get home."

"*Hmpft!* We'll see about squaring up this kind'a thing *if* and when we get home. Right now, I'm hungry. So...let's go eat. They must'a opened up the dining room by now." She heads for the door while George pats his Nikon and slowly puts it back in the case, then follows her.

George and Brenda climb up the stairs towards the dining room, where they seat themselves next to a window, as they are the first passengers to enter and no serving people are yet around. It's dark outside; all they can see out the window is an occasional bit of white foam topping the waves, illuminated by lights from the ship. Unexpectedly, a large woman comes in and asserts herself over their table.

"Excuse me," she commands. "This is the captain's table. The captain is my husband. It's reserved."

"Oh," says George, "if this is your table, we'll get another right away," and he looks around to see where he and Brenda could move.

"Look lady," says Brenda, "there's four other tables by the window. Why can't you sit at one of them? I've already drunk some water out of this glass." And she holds up the glass to show that she has imprinted it with her red lipstick.

"Take the glass with you," says George to Brenda. He's already on his feet, and to the woman he says, "So sorry, we didn't know there was reserved seats."

Brenda slowly gets up and, glaring at the woman, moves over to another table by a window.

"George," she says, after they seat themselves, "why on earth couldn't ya show some spunk? That old nag doesn't have to push us around like that. Why d'ja let her?"

"I didn't want to make trouble the first night we're out. We're on this boat for a week, ya know."

"Jeez, George, sometimes you make me sick. Oh well, let's see what they got to eat." And she opens her menu, as a pretty, friendly waitress comes by and refills the water glasses and asks where is home for them and hopes they've brought enough warm clothes.

*   *   *

The ship plows on through the night, engines throbbing heavily. At one point there's a bit of rough water, and in her bunk Brenda complains about her stomach. "I think I'm seasick, George. Get up and get me some of those seasick pills, won't ya?"

George is sleeping soundly, having dreamt a half-asleep, half-awake dream about the pretty waitress who served them dinner, but he rolls dutifully out of his bunk when he hears Brenda's voice and staggers to the bathroom, where he finds the pills and hands them to her.

"How'm I supposed to swallow a pill without water?"

And George staggers to the bathroom again and gets her a glass of water. She swallows the pill, passes gas and rolls over with her side away from him, moaning, "I hope that does the trick."

* * *

In the early morning, George gets up and dresses in his warmest clothes without waking Brenda. He slips his Nikon around his neck and heads for the deck. As he opens the heavy door leading out, a blast of very cold air hits him in the face, almost reminding him of the long-ago days of snowball fights.

"*Whup!*" he says to himself in reaction to both. But the sight before his eyes is astounding. It seems to be a world of nothing but blues and grays—blues and grays of all shades and tones, and the brightest white he has ever seen, glinting off the ice. And the air, there is something about the air that is cold for sure, but invigorating...pure. And the clouds, they are as strange as the ice formations. He pulls out his Nikon and starts shooting images of icebergs or clouds, immersed in their strange formations and shapes, one after the other.

"Gawd," he thinks, "what will the boys back home say about all of this!"

Brenda finally gets up, dresses herself in what she hopes are warm but stylish clothes and wanders up to the deck, where she finds George, still taking pictures as the ship winds its way among the islands of the Antarctica Peninsula.

"So that's where you are! C'mon George, stop taking pictures! Breakfast will be over and we'll miss it if you don't hurry." She pulls at the sleeve of his old L.L. Bean parka.

"I'll be there in a minute. You go on ahead. There's just too much to see here, and Brenda, take a big, deep breath of this air. It will do your lungs good after all them cigarettes you smoke."

Brenda acts as if deaf, turns toward the heavy door, pulls it open with a lot of effort and slams it behind her.

Later that day and on every subsequent day after breakfast, George climbs into a rubber Zodiac exploration boat with the other passengers to go up close to some of the icebergs and perhaps land on a beach, should they find a colony of penguins. Brenda elects to stay on board. She spends her time wandering back and forth between their stateroom, the lounge and the little library, where she tries to read. She finds that every passenger has gone off to look at the scenery. She goes on deck, which is too cold for her, but it is the only place aboard where smoking is allowed. She's bored, her stomach's still not quite right, in fact her whole body seems to be tied up in one mess of knots. "What *am* I doing here?" she says to herself over and over.

George comes back with the others at lunchtime. They are full of stories. There has been a sighting of a whale, there were a few penguins on a far shore, they've seen and heard glaciers crack and huge chunks of ice fall from one of them into the sea, making a noise like thunder.

"That's called 'calving,' you know, and them little pieces of ice floating around are called 'bergy bits,' and I saw seals sitting on them!" George explains to Brenda, his excitement hardly contained as he views his efforts on his new camera.

"Wait 'til you see what pictures I've taken, Brenda. Oh...you gotta go with me tomorrow, we're goin' to where the guide knows there's a big colony of penguins. Adelie penguins, the really cute ones...oh, you just gotta come and see them! And, by the way, Harriet has asked us to have drinks with her up in the lounge tonight before dinner."

"Who's Harriet?"

"Harriet's quite the gal. She's my new friend. Remember her asking us to move from the table one night?"

Brenda says, "Oh, the big bossy one! Who said she was the captain's wife…Hah! Why'd you make a friend of her, for heaven's sake?" But she goes to the lounge with George and listens stony-faced while he and Harriet chatter over their adventures ashore, wishing she could at least have a cigarette.

After other passengers urge her to join them on the exploration boat the next day—during the night the crew will move the ship to yet another position, a place where there is supposed to be a large penguin colony— she agrees, remembering that she's always thought penguins were cute.

She is fearful as she steps onto the rubber Zodiac, even with the help of the nature guide. They head towards a stony beach below huge rock cliffs, covered with layers of moss and lichens. Above the cliffs are massive amounts of snow and ice. The rubber boat lands on the beach, and Brenda is the last to leave. She is repelled by the pungent odor from the penguin colony filling the air, but she carefully steps out onto the stones. George, meanwhile, is among the first to disembark and is already way up ahead, hurrying and stumbling over stones, and snapping pictures of the little creatures, who remain unafraid of these big things that have just landed, looking like they have only one eye.

The guide is talking about the birds: how they are

very social; how there are only seventeen species; how they have remained virtually unchanged for the last forty-five million years; how they spend eighty-five percent of their lives at sea; how their short, stubby wings are adapted so they can fly through the water; how they get around on land by propping themselves up on their stubby tails and waddle, or lie down and toboggan around on their stomachs, kicking with their feet and paddling with their wings. A group of very attentive passengers listens carefully to him amid the cacophony of the penguins. The birds are commenting noisily to one another about the arrival of these beings.

Brenda tries to listen to the guide, but she can't hear well. And she wants a cigarette but there is no way she can smoke one, so bundled up in heavy coat, gloves, scarf and hat, and fearful of the probable scorn of her vigorous fellow passengers. George is intent, listens for a while and then leaves to take more shots of the birds and the terrain. Brenda drags herself after him and, groaning, stumbles, nearly falling down over some stones as, without warning, a cheeky penguin pops up from his crowd, waddles over to an off-balance Brenda and takes a nip at her leg. She cries out but no one hears her. The penguin retreats, looking satisfied, as Brenda lurches back to the guide, only her pride injured.

"Why didn't you tell us those damned birds might bite?" she demands of him. The guide only laughs and says, "Well, you should have listened to me. I told the other passengers that this can happen sometimes."

Brenda is furious and, inside her gloved hand, gives the finger to the guide. Her stomach churns, her mind is again one great, big, red patch...angry at George, the constant wind, the cold, the scenery, the smelly penguins, the earnest passengers, the polite but self-important guides. Even the cheery young crew members annoy her as they help her off the Zodiac on return to the ship.

The cruise is coming to an end. This last night aboard, the passengers are full of high spirits. They drink and eat dinner as newfound companions, telling tales about their various exploits on the Antarctic Peninsula islands. George is having a real good a time with Harriet, who knows everyone and whose bawdy humor has everyone laughing and chattering together. "They remind me of that smelly bunch of birds," Brenda thinks.

No one notices that she slips away to the cabin, where she looks for and finds George's Nikon in his carefully packed suitcase. She removes it from its case and puts the case back, empty, in the suitcase. Then she sneaks back upstairs. She opens the heavy door to the deck. She walks over to the railing and drops the camera into the sea. She pulls out a cigarette, lights it and, for the first time in a week, smiles. She leans up against the heavy door as the ship makes its way back to Punta Arenas, Chile.

But what she didn't know was that before dinner, George transferred all of his pictures to his new iPad Mini, a real secret from Brenda. Here they would be safely stored, just in case something unfortunate came along.

The Dinner Party

A long time ago, I was invited to a dinner party by the neighbors who lived nearby. I was in South Carolina then, intending to sell the house that my husband and I had bought.

It had been our pleasant home for many winters, but his doctor had told him that what with his heart trouble, it would be best for him if he left the thirty-degree-below temperatures that often occur in wintertime Vermont.

I was alone there in Springville to sell the house, as no one else in my family had time to do so—my husband had died the previous summer. That evening, I dressed with care, as this Southern couple looked to me always so put-together in stylish clothes, appropriate for whatever occasion they found themselves in. Clothes, for me, mean nothing more than just something to cover me up or keep me warm. I feel that I have no fashion sense at all, and I don't particularly care. But that evening, I put on my one and only best dress (luckily I had thought to pack it), a black number—of what material I had no idea—but it had a high neck and long sleeves to cover up all my close-to-aging flab. In it, I always felt secure.

When I arrived, everyone had already gathered and they were drinking cocktails, as was the custom there. I do not drink any alcohol and was offered, amid a certain amount of derision, a glass of seltzer with a bit of ice.

A maid came in to announce that dinner was ready, and we all filed into the large dining room, where an antique table was set with gleaming old silver on crisp white and costly linen, sparkling crystal, many glasses at each place. In the center of the table was a huge silver bowl filled with a perfect arrangement of pink, white and red camellias and scented jasmine.

At each end of the table sat the host and hostess. Opposite me was my good friend Bee, a petite, blonde Southerner with terrific liberal and funny ideas. She had married Frank, a Yankee, who had adopted the South because of the fun he could have, just messing about on his fishing boat or taking his single-man shell out on the river to row up and down in complete, happy retirement abandon. Bee, meanwhile, was head-over-heels in environmental causes—democratic politics, educational opportunities for needy kids, all things that I was engaged in but never able to match Bee's ability to speak her mind so skillfully.

Bee's husband was seated on my right, and on my left was Greg, a Swedish professor who had come over to teach Nordic literature to the retirees in an organization for senior learners, in a branch of the big state university. It was conveniently located just up the street. Most of us were, or had been, attending a class or two there. Also across the table was Mariestar, a self-named artist. She had a studio downtown where she sold flamboyant clothing, along with her paintings, which not many bought. She was a kind of flaky character, but nice, I always thought. Next to her and on Bee's right was Stanley.

Stanley was supposed to have made millions either in the stock market or building cell phone towers or trading with Arabs. No one really knew. But he was buying up most of the run-down property in this little old Southern town and was rumored to have amazing plans for it all, although no one then had seen any results. I, frankly, couldn't stand the sight of the man; he was overweight, with a red-veined nose and squinty eyes. I hoped that when I put my house on the market, he wouldn't be the one who made the first offer. I looked at him and saw that he chewed his food with his mouth open. *Yuck!*

The dinner conversation opened by the hostess asking if anyone had seen a good movie. All of the guests seemed then to ruminate over this remark, along with sipping their she-crab soup and munching on delicate cheese wafers, so no one said anything until Stanley piped up with, "Hell! Who has time to go to the movies anyway?"

Bee replied. "Stanley. I just saw Al Gore's movie, *An Inconvenient Truth*. It was alarming. Everyone should go and see it. In my opinion, it's quite wonderful."

"Yah," said Professor Greg, who had been trying to put his hand on my knee all through the soup course and me trying to remove it, politely but firmly. "In Sveden, it goes over big-time."

"That'd be just like you Svedes," said Stanley, in poor imitation of Professor Greg's accent. "The most licentious, depraved lot on earth—all you Scandihoovians!"

Stanley, obviously, had already had too much to drink. But Bee, true to form, was not going to let him get away with this comment. She jumped right in. "Stanley, for heaven's sake, apologize to the professor. I'm ashamed of you."

Stanley said nothing to her or the professor and continued to slurp his soup in a most unattractive way, staring at the tablecloth.

The host broke the tension by asking, "Bee, what did you find so important about this film? Maybe you could explain it to all us know-nothings."

I had only seen the host once or twice walking by my house, taking his three boys out fishing. I had no idea what he did for a living, really nothing much more about him except that he looked pleasant and genial, with a slight Southern drawl.

Bee was ready. She turned toward Stanley and said, "In this film, Gore explains about global warming. He has scientific proof that we have added to—perhaps only a natural change on earth—a huge amount of carbon dioxide, CO_2 it is known popularly, into the atmosphere, which causes the greenhouse effect."

"So, what's so bad about that?"

"It makes like a blanket over the earth," Bee replied, "It traps the sun's heat and makes the earth warm up."

"Again I ask," (Stanley talked with his mouth full of food as well, I saw) "what's so bad about that? I'm here to get warm anyway. Kansas winters are ba-a-a-d; I'd go back if it were warmer there. At least in Kansas there aren't so many bleeding hearts as there are in this town."

"That's because so many of you Yankees have come down here as snowbirds," said our host, looking at Bee's husband and me, and winking at us.

"Yes," said Frank, Bee's husband, "and you told me

once that I was all right, but to make sure to close the gate after me and not let any more of us in." He did not wink back.

Mary, the hostess, waved her hands with fancily manicured, red-tipped nails. "Oh, dee-yuh, let's not go theyuh…. Go back to Gore's film, Bee. What all else did y'all discover? Ah think it all so's important." She had always kept her Texas drawl and never spoke like a South Carolinian even though she had been married to Robert for twenty-five years or more, she once told me.

The maid came in with plates of a very colorful entrée. It was a delicious shrimp, tomato and spicy rice dish with bright green asparagus, set off by sweet potato soufflé. For a while conversation lagged as we ate.

Stanley had been thinking over Gore's movie, and started talking again at Bee. "So, Bee, I suppose Gore thinks the USA is the biggest contributor to global warming—like through our cars and stuff. I'm not going to give up my Caddy just for the sake of his cock-a-ninny ideas!"

Bee, startled a bit by his outburst, jerked back in her seat, but said quietly to him, "You have that one right, Stanley. We have. Just from folks,"—here she hesitated a bit—"like you, who drive the most horrible, big, gas-guzzling cars and think nothing about how this might affect the rest of the world. Right now, we are the worst polluters on earth."

"Come on, Bee," said Frank, "That's a pretty strong statement. I guess I should have gone to this movie with you."

Stanley exploded, "American technology can take care of anything. So what if we are polluting? I don't care. We'll fix it if it gets serious. Anyway, Gore exaggerates for the sake of publicity. He's just mad because he got beat and's not president."

Stanley signaled the maid for more wine. She poured it for him and he drank up the wine in a couple of gulps.

Mariestar, a good friend of our hostess, had not said anything so far. But now she looked at Stanley and said, "I *suppose*, Stanley, you haven't read much about this frightening prospect for the world. I *suppose* business hasn't let you had the time."

Mariestar's outfit was a bit odd, I thought. She had on black pants and a gauzy, multicolored top—from her store maybe—and had wrapped her head in a kind of matching turban, finished off with wearing long, dangling earrings, clanking bracelets and huge rings on most of her fingers. My guess was that in dressing herself, she wanted to create a very arty look, compared to the rest of us plainer folk.

Stanley looked at her as if she was some kind of bug or something of no consequence and said, "You got that right, babe."

He signaled the maid again, who was clearing the

plates, for more wine, and then said, "And what's so frightening anyway, if the world warms up?"

Bee was patient. "Scientists say that the glaciers will melt, and in some places like in Greenland, they already are. The oceans are warming and this will bring on more serious storms, to say nothing about losing coral reefs where many fish live."

I could see that Bee was only just warming up, and I wondered if the host and hostess were ready to referee, should an argument ensue. Fortunately, dessert arrived in the form of crème brulée, and that got the attention of all assembled—at least for a while.

After dinner, we all went back into the living room and the maid came in with little cups of very hot, strong black coffee.

"Not to worry, y'all," said Mary. "It's decaf. So after a little taste of this special brew, y'all can sleep like babies once you're home." We laughed, and Stanley, who had been quiet and looked sour after his dinner table outburst, smiled, took a cup of coffee and announced it delicious. Then, leaning on the chair arms, he got up unsteadily and said he had to go home early, as he was flying out tomorrow on a mission to look at some possible oil drilling sites somewhere in Alaska. He said, with a smirk, "I hope that doesn't distress you, Bee. It's in conservation land up there somewhere."

"Of course that should distress *everyone*, Stanley.

How stupid is that!" This came from Mariestar, even before Bee could open her mouth in surprise. Mariestar continued. "I really cannot understand people like you, Stanley. You want to wreck everything that is beautiful on this earth just for the sake of, of making *money*! It just makes me *sick*." Her face was turning red in anger.

Stanley ignored Mariestar's comments. "Thank you," he said to Mary and Robert, "it was a delicious dinner," and tottered out the front door.

Mary said, "Ah sure hope that man gets on home awright. He seems a bit tipsy to me." Agreeing with her comment, we continued to talk pleasantly together for a while until I looked at my watch and saw that it was nearly midnight.

"Oh, my goodness," I said, "Here it is way past my bedtime. I've really got to go, as the woman from the real estate company is coming tomorrow early and I better be up and ready for her."

Professor Greg offered to walk me home, as his apartment was just beyond my house. At first, I demurred, thinking about his wandering hand, but he seemed to have realized I was not interested in whatever it was he had in mind. So I agreed, we said our goodbyes, and went down the long flight of stairs onto the street. It was very dark, and I was actually glad to have some company on my ten-minute walk home. We lived in a part of Springville where just about everyone walked to get places.

We chatted a bit about the dinner party as we walked along, the professor announcing with no uncertainty that he thought Stanley a complete boob, with which I agreed. Few people were still up in the neighborhood. Not only was it dark, it was very quiet, the rustle of the breeze off the river making the only sound as it blew through the tops of the palms and live oaks. It was indeed a lovely place in which to live, and I think the professor must have been thinking similar thoughts, as he said, "This town is magical for me. Ve have nothing like it in Sveden. It vould be so very nice if every year I vas here to teach for a semester—especially now, in spring—so very beautiful."

"Well-named town, Springville," I said.

True, daffodils came out in late February. There was a place on one of the barrier islands where there were fields and fields of them. Once you could go over there and, for a dollar, pick as many as your arms could hold.

People had camellias and azaleas, all shades of pink, white, orange and red, in bloom around their houses and gardens. Purple wisteria had gone wild, roping itself throughout even the tallest trees, the scent wafting down to you whenever there was the slightest breeze.

Both the professor and I were caught up in some sort of dreamlike walk. It was nice that he wasn't the chatty sort that could have disturbed my total enchantment.

But, we both came about abruptly by a strange sound in the bushes, "You hear that?" the professor stopped, "Listen, vill you, and tell me vhat iss."

I listened. Surely, there were strange sounds coming from some thick bushes that we had just passed, sort of grunts and then a rustling sound and more grunt-like noises.

"I have a very small flashlight in my purse. Let me see if it still works," I said, and fished around in my purse for it. It produced a very dim light.

"Here, lady," said the professor. "Let me have it and I will see vhat iss. Please...step aside."

I gave it to him and he turned its very weak light on where the noise was coming from. I could hear faint groans now, as we both approached the sound, and then a faint "Help me, please, help me." We both stopped instantly and the professor shone the feeble light on where these words were coming from. It was Stanley. He lay squirming in the bushes, covered with vomit, leaves and dirt, a small stick protruded from one of his eyes. Obvious signs showed us that he had fallen into the bushes and somehow a woody stem had broken off in his fall and pierced his eyeball.

"Oh, my God!" Both the professor and I said in utter horror.

"I'll get over to that house as fast as I can," said the professor, pointing to a house that still was showing a light from an upstairs window, "and get an ambulance. You stay here with Stanley."

I stood in the street, watching him run to the house and hearing Stanley's moans. The professor obviously couldn't take much more of this scene. But he was efficient—as I stood there trying to reassure Stanley that he would be all right soon, I could hear the ambulance sirens, and the blue lights of a police car soon appeared around the corner.

"I hope you can hear those sounds, Stanley," I said loudly, thinking these words might give him some comfort, but Stanley just groaned in agony, as blood continued to gush down his face from his wounded eye.

The EMS crew, without any look of distress on the faces of these people who had to deal with Stanley's condition, quickly bundled him onto a gurney, shoved him into the back of the ambulance and, with sirens screeching, took him away to the hospital.

The professor and I walked slowly home. "What an ending to a kind of amazing evening," I said to him, as I stood in front of my house. "Thank you so much for walking back with me. I am ever so grateful that you were with me." I started to shake hands with him.

The professor bowed, took my extended hand and kissed it—so old-fashioned and continental. "Good night," he said cheerfully, "Let's hope Stanley survives. I vouldn't vish anything else on him, even though he's total *drek!*"

I never saw the professor again. I sold my house to a woman from Baltimore, packed up all my belongings and went home to Vermont, my favorite place in the whole world.

* * *

So many changes as the years flew by. I heard that my glorious, funny friend Bee had died. The neighbors whose dinner party I had attended had moved to Charleston; in fact, it sounded as if the whole neighborhood had changed, and not for the better, as even the senior learning center had moved away.

One day I took the train to New York City. I was going to there to visit an old school friend. I figured I had better do it when I could still manage to get on and off the train, or not get confused or lost in the depths of Penn Station once I had arrived. I was anxious to go, even though this might be my last time. My friend lived in a grand Park Avenue apartment and told me she had all kinds of tickets to the latest Broadway plays and we would make a visit or two to the city's fabulous museums.

I had moved from Vermont to be closer to my daughter in Massachusetts and had bought a small house in one of Boston's suburbs. I was going to New York from the Route 128 station. I like train trips and even though it was lots cheaper to go by bus, I chose the train, probably for sentimental reasons, remembering those wonderful trips to New York with my parents when I was young.

I watched the scenery go by. It hadn't changed much, the big cedar swamp flashed by in southern Massachusetts and soon we were rolling along the seaside in Connecticut, where I saw some swans, so wonderfully white against the blue ocean. Near New Haven, we had to get out while the train switched over to electricity.

At one of the last stops before New York, two men got on and sat down on the last remaining seats, which were right behind me. I couldn't help but overhear their conversation, since they talked with intensity about their trip to Maine, where they had been involved in testing out a new wind turbine blade that was lighter and more efficient than anything else that had been developed.

One of them, in an older-sounding voice, said, "Yes. I know we have a long way to go before the U.S. population in general adopts these ideas. But we've got to do something bold to develop alternate sources of energy. And making some of these things will certainly help the returning, unemployed war veterans."

The other man answered him, saying, "You certainly have been beating this drum for a long while, haven't you? For sources of alternate energy, that is."

"That's right, Bill," the older voice answered, "But this was a long time in coming through to me. I guess I really have to thank my wife for this change. She was the only one—out of the many friends I *thought* I had there—who came to visit me in the hospital after I had that ghastly accident I've already told you about. She came every day, and as I got better, we just fell into a relationship that I have thanked the gods above for, every day of my life. She gave me like...a velvet lecture every day about preserving what was beautiful and how she thought so many people were thoughtlessly destroying our little blue planet. She kept talking about 'our little blue planet' and how we must all care for it, and *how* we should care for it..."

"Well," said the other voice, "I've been told that artists are known to be prescient. And I'm glad that she has been so successful, both with you *and* her art." He was cheerful as he talked.

"Yes," said the older voice, "and I have helped her get established in some of the finest galleries around the world."

I was interested that he wasn't boasting about being such a patron of art. He seemed only to be surprised that this woman's art had so taken the world by storm.

I have always thought it rude to turn around and see who's talking behind you, especially if you find yourself in a public place like a train. But my curiosity got the better of me. I just had to see who these men were, since it pleased me to hear what they were saying. I decided to get up and go into the café car for some coffee, and as I passed by the seat where the two men were sitting, I noticed that one of them, an older fellow, was wearing a patch over one eye.

And then an astounding thought overcame me. Could it possibly be *Stanley*? Was the woman, the wife whom he was talking about, could that possibly have been *Mariestar*? My mind was taking me back to the dinner party and its gruesome aftermath. No...not likely, no...it couldn't be, I thought. My weird mind just had to be playing tricks on me. But again curiosity won. I came back to my seat with my coffee. And I just had to stop in front of them, while watching all the tall towers of Manhattan come into view, quite a beautiful sight in the twilight of this day.

"Excuse me," I said to them, looking right at the man who was wearing the eye patch. "Is your name, by any chance, Stanley Goddard?"

The man wearing the eye patch looked up and with a little smile on his face asked, "And just who is it that wants to know?"

Could it be? Was it possibly...the voice—and face— of a much older Stanley Goddard?

I said, "My name is Jean, Jean Ross. You might

remember me from living in Springville, South Carolina...now quite a few years ago. We were at a dinner party together and when you were hurt, it was the professor and I who found you in the bushes and called the ambulance."

"I'm sorry Miss...or is it Mrs.? I'm afraid I can't help you. I never was in *any* Springville in my life. I have no such recollection." And he turned away from me to look out the window.

"Please, lady," said the man sitting next to Stanley. "Please. Do not bother us with any more questions. Go, sit down with your coffee and drink it before it gets too cold."

I could not help but be puzzled about this strange possibility. I sat down with my coffee as the train plunged down into the tunnel for Penn Station. Stony silence passed between us until our destination was reached. Leaving the train, I soon lost them in the crowd.

Hair #2

Two people, a tall, handsome man and an equally handsome but smaller, stylish, gray-haired woman were seated in the dining room at Eggleston Manor, a retirement community. They were engaged in what looked like a very intimate conversation.

The man had just enough gray hair at the temples to give him a distinguished, worldly look. He was wearing a navy blue blazer, striped tie and standard gray flannel pants. Sipping a glass of cabernet, he listened intensely to the woman, who was dressed in a silky, beige pantsuit with just enough gold jewelry, illustrating a certain venerable sartorial splendor.

He said, smiling at her, "It's so nice to see you in such good health, with such an upbeat point of view and still so easy to talk to, after all these years of me being out of the country." His teeth were a sparkling white when he smiled.

She replied, "Well, thank you, Steven. I elected to move here so that I wouldn't become a burden on anyone. But living here reminds me of my college years, as we have to agree to certain standards, a little bit foolish in my opinion at times...like telling the administration if we're going to be gone for just one night! And I don't like the looks of this gadget around my wrist—we have to wear them in case we fall and can't get up. On the whole, though, I'm surrounded by pleasant people and I've made some very nice new friends." When she smiled, her teeth were not dazzling white like his.

Looking around the room, the man asked, "Why in the world are there so many blondes in this place? Quite a change from where I've been, I can tell you. If women dyed their hair there, it was usually a strange purplish color." He was looking puzzled.

Savoring this most pleasurable moment of putting her hand on his and giving it a gentle squeeze, she said, "Few people around here use henna. Gray or graying hair is easy to turn blonde."

"Do they think this makes them look younger—even with a face full of wrinkles?"

"Do you see that man over there?" She pointed a sneaky and somewhat arthritic finger at a stout man who had dyed his hair a garish yellow-orange and had made a valiant, but not exactly successful, effort to cover a big bald spot.

"He's trying for the Donald Trump effect, so it's not only women who do this trying-to-stay-young thing. I'm told he even dyes his eyebrows!" She made a disgusted face.

At this remark, the man laughed heartily and, lifting his glass of wine, said, "Please, don't you ever dye your hair! I wouldn't know you and I wouldn't like it. After all, you are my very special grandma!"

The woman smiled again and continued to hold on tightly to her grandson's hand.

Subtraction

It is an unusually hot summer day for midcoast Maine. Sarah, age eighty-nine, is going for a swim. She's walking ever so slowly and carefully over rough ground now, watching out for treacherously embedded stones and tree roots that lie in the path, ready to trip up any unwary traveler. The path leads to the dock, where rowboats are tied next to a fixed swimming ladder.

Sarah has vacationed on Summer Island since she was a baby, and her time there follows a routine that is customary for many of the regular summer "rusticators," as the island people call the summer people. Sarah had brought her own children to Summer Island every year, and now they were in the process of bringing their children when they had time.

Sarah could spend the whole summer there in her

little cottage by the tidal creek. This morning, she had spent hours trying to decide on a bathing suit that might fit. Age had played a mean trick in changing her body horizontally and longitudinally. But this was the day she was determined to swim.

It might even be the last one, she'd reflected as she surveyed herself in the mirror after deciding on an ancient black number, a Speedo from years ago, when she had enrolled in a water exercise class.

"Ugh," she said to her image. "I guess you aren't telling me anything I don't already know...such flabby, shapeless, pale and wrinkled skin with lumps and bumps that have appeared from nowhere."

Hurriedly, she slipped on a big pink shirt and headed out the door.

It is high tide. There is no wind. Spruce and fir trees mirror themselves in the slick, dark, almost oily-appearing water. As Sarah makes her careful way down the gangplank, she is greeted by an assortment of surprised young relatives, swimming and sunning themselves on big beach towels spread out all over the dock. She hears many comments about her appearance as a potential swimmer and many suggestions offered on how she should get into the water.

Smiling, she listens to them all. She thinks about what they are saying and, angered, decides to do just the opposite. She thinks, *These people have no idea that I was once a very good swimmer, and I'm not going to be like old Cousin Anna, crawling fearfully down the ladder and having to be pulled out when she found the water way too cold.*

Instead, with this forced bravado, she peels off the big shirt, strides to the edge of the dock and dives in amid a chorus of astonished onlookers.

After executing a neat but not spectacular dive, she surfaces, to find her body shaking. Salt water stings her eyes and nostrils as it streams down her face, and she gasps for air. She tries a few tentative strokes, hoping to regain her stability, becoming aware of the sticky, salty water on her skin, which is making it itchy. She can hear her relatives on the dock yelling to her with frightened cries. "Are you all right?" "Don't swim out too far!" "Do you need help?"

She turns over to float on her back and gives them a wobbly thumbs-up, hoping it is enough to reassure them. The buoyancy of her body and the warmth of the top layer of water bring her back to the fun she had with her sisters and cousins, paddling about in the water after it had been warmed by hours of the hot summer sun, now so many, many summers ago. She even closes her eyes, thinking about those happy times. When a little breeze begins to ripple the water, she decides she should head towards the dock before she gets cold. She will climb up the swimming ladder and sit in the sun, briefly—now that she is aware of its cancer-giving properties—until she dries off.

Grabbing the ladder in both hands, she puts her left leg on the lowest rung and tries to pull herself up. Funny...it seems very, very difficult. She puts her right leg on the rung and again tries pulling herself up, amid encouraging cheers from those on the dock. But no matter how hard she tries, she cannot get herself up and out of the water. Her legs are like jelly, neither of them strong enough to support her weight, even though she recently lost twenty pounds. One big fellow says he'll pull her out if she can just stand on the ladder. He tries, but she falls back into the water.

"Never mind trying to help me anymore," she says, her teeth chattering like castanets. "I'll just swim around to the beach and get out there."

Now she's really cold. Swimming as quickly as she can, she makes her way through masses of slippery seaweed fronds until she feels the rocky beach under her toes. Like a seal, or really more like an old sea walrus, she thinks—she hauls herself up out of the water and tries to stand. The rocks roll under her feet and she falls backward into the water, nicking her elbows on rocks.

Now on hands and knees, she manages to crawl onto the beach, and tries once again to stand. Very difficult, with the smooth, round stones rolling around beneath her feet and causing her to lose her balance time and time again.

At the edge of the beach, on the bank, Sarah sees a thoughtful relative holding a long, sturdy stick, her pink shirt and her shoes.

"Sarah!" she calls. "I'll throw this stick to you. It will help. I'm not coming down there though, as I know I would fall."

"Thank you!" Sarah calls out to her as she retrieves the stick. "That was a good shot, Barbara, and I'm grateful, let me tell you!"

She makes her way slowly over the loose stones, dried, stinky seaweed and beach detritus. Her bathing suit is now an uncomfortable itchy presence; she looks down at her legs, noting the many bloody spots, and ruefully says to herself, *Those will take months to heal, what with my awful, old-lady skin!*

She makes her hurried way back to the cottage, showers and applies Band-Aids to all the little cuts on her legs. She puts on an old Vermont Country Store muumuu and fixes herself an iced tea with lots of lemon and ice. Sitting down on one of the plastic chairs on the deck facing the creek, she breathes a sigh of relief.

"Well, Sarah! That misadventure tells you it's one more thing you used to do that must be crossed off the list," she says to no one in particular. "And another: If Tom were here, we'd be sitting right here—but drinking gin and tonics."

She raises her glass of tea. "*Salud*, Tom!" she says to the air. Sitting down again, she says, "One more item to scratch off the list...I wonder what's next."

The Houses and Other Stories
is formatted in the
Chaparral Pro font family